Raptor's REVENGE

ROYAL BASTARDS MC

EST 2019

USA TODAY BESTELLING AUTHOR
KRISTINE ALLEN

To Glenna… because you're a badass b*tch—Author, Cover Designer, and the bomb-diggity of friends. You freaking rock!

Note To Readers

Raptor's Revenge is a continuation of *Taming Raptor*. While it might still make sense as a standalone book, it is recommended *Taming Raptor* be read first to avoid confusion. That will give you the entire picture of events that led up to this story. Enjoy!

Raptor's REVENGE

ROYAL BASTARDS MC

ONE

Raptor

"BEG"—SEETHER

Silverware scraped on the plates as everyone finished their food. Sam and Seth had stayed at the clubhouse last night, then helped with construction today. Sage had cooked, and we were all sitting at the single round table that fit in the clubhouse kitchen. It was the closest thing to home and a family dinner that I could provide at the moment. Though I hadn't been able to raise the boys for most of their lives, it irked me to feel like I wasn't properly providing them a stable place to chill.

In a way, I regretted my decision to sink the majority of my money into the RBMC property by buying it from the club. It would've been ideal if I had bought a house close by, but at the time, I had no idea things would play out the way they did.

Seth leaned back in his chair and placed a hand on his flat stomach, then rubbed circles on it. "Sage, I'm so full, but that was delicious."

Sage cocked a brow at his action with a teasing smirk. "Are you making fun of me?" she asked as she mimicked his action by placing a hand on her now obviously rounded stomach. She'd just started to really show, and I couldn't believe what a turn-on it was. I'd never been into pregnant chicks before, but with Sage I was at half-mast any time I laid my eyes on her.

Sam snickered and shoveled his last bite in his mouth.

"Can we stay here again tonight?" Seth asked with pleading eyes. I frowned, and he glanced down at his empty plate, obviously mistaking my expression. "Ms. Ackerman is out of town this week, and Mom doesn't get back until next week."

"Where's your mom this time?" I tried to sound casual and keep the censure from my tone because that wasn't fair to them.

He shrugged. "No clue. Out of the country with Hatham again."

"Jesus. How often do they go out of the country?" It seemed like they were gone every other week, though I'd figured out it was about once a month, sometimes two. It was hard to keep my hatred for their mother out of our interactions. She took my children from me, lied to me, got a restraining order against me, then essentially abandoned the children she went to so much trouble to take. What was the point? To punish me because I didn't do what she expected of me?

Yes.

He rolled his eyes. "All the time."

"What the fuck for?" Okay, maybe my response wasn't super tactful, but it was a struggle. Every. Fucking. Day.

"I don't know. Hatham has a lot of international businesses he deals with—Mom shops," Sam explained with a roll of his eyes.

Seth remained quiet with his gaze locked on his empty plate.

"It's gonna suck after Ms. Ackerman retires. I wish we could live with you," Seth mumbled.

"Seth!" Sam hissed, and I glanced between them before I let out a laugh that was more designed to show the boys I wasn't upset about anything Seth said. Sage remained quiet, yet watched everything unfolding.

I couldn't help but wonder if he really meant it or if he was simply angry at his mother and venting. It was hard to ask without talking shit about her—no matter how much I wanted to do exactly that.

"And leave your big mansion to live in a cabin that's probably smaller than your bedroom there?" I teased, watching him closely as I seethed inside.

"Yes."

Silence was a suffocating weight in the room.

My attempt at joking ended as my chest clenched and my heart raced. My gaze darted between the boys, then to Sage. Her wide-eyed stare told me she was as shocked as I

3

was. Though I'd been spending a lot of time with the boys, never in a million years would I have thought they would want to live with me. Since I didn't have a lot to offer them, I never would've asked.

I considered my words carefully while I tapped the tabletop in agitation.

After I swallowed the baseball lodged in my throat, I asked them, "If I could make that happen, you'd want to live here? Knowing I can't offer you the luxuries they can? Because if your answer is yes, I will do everything in my power in a heartbeat."

My family had money. After sinking my savings into the property, I certainly didn't. Yet none of us was anywhere near Hatham's level.

The boys looked at each other and an unspoken conversation seemed to pass between them. Their expressions told me this was something they'd discussed before. Sam sat up straight and looked me square in the eye.

"Yes, sir," he boldly replied. Seth mimicked his actions with a nod.

I gave a huff of disbelief and fell back in my chair. No matter how much I liked to think I was a badass motherfucker, these two humbled me. And blew me away. They could've grown up to absolutely hate me, but no matter how angry Sam was when he found me again, he ensured Seth didn't hold a grudge or have hate in his heart for me.

It was a gift that not only showed what a big heart he had, it was also a selfless act that I couldn't begin to repay.

I regretted that I didn't push harder—but I'd been

devastated and felt like I couldn't trust a soul—not even my own fucking family. Falina had done that in one fell swoop. Stolen my children, destroyed my soul and my trust in women, and divided me from my family. I'd never felt more alone in my life than I did back then. Which was probably why the RBMC filled that gaping hole in me and filled the family void. They were there for me when I believed no one else was.

"Then I'll make it happen."

They never need to know how I do that.

I sat in the dark, enjoying a glass of the expensive scotch I'd helped myself to. It went down smooth, and I considered taking the bottle. The front door opened, and I heard the click of heels on the marble floors, then the quiet sound of the security system being cleared and reset. Though she needn't have bothered.

The tall, elegant silhouette moved into the living room, and I silently waited.

When the lamp illuminated the room, I enjoyed the shriek that slipped from her lips. Her hand splayed over her chest, and the massive diamond glittered in the low light.

"Adrien!" she gasped. "What are you doing here?"

Without saying a word, I lifted the golden liquid to my lips and enjoyed the rich taste as it crossed my tongue and went down. Evidently, it was what millions of dollars afforded you—the finest whiskey. Then, as if I had all the time in the world, I set it on the glossy table by the side of my chair.

Elbows on the arms of the luxurious leather, I steepled my fingers and continued to stare.

"Where is Ms. Ackerman—and the boys?" she asked. It was as if she was finally realizing there was no one else in the home.

"Out" was my clipped reply as she took a few tentative steps toward me.

Wariness flickered in her eyes, halting her progress. "H-how did you get in here?"

Ahhh, the fear is starting to settle in—as it should.

"Does it matter?"

Her throat bobbed as she swallowed.

"Have a seat, Falina," I instructed with a misleading pleasantness in my tone.

"I think I'd rather—" she began, but I cut her off.

"Sit! The! Fuck! Down!" I roared, and she immediately dropped into the chair across from me.

"Adrien." She called my name in an almost plea-like whisper.

"Do you know how bad I want to wrap my fingers around your throat? How clearly I can imagine you gasping for your last breath as you claw at my unrelenting hands?" My fingers twitched at the thought.

As if she could imagine it as well, she lifted one hand to protectively span her neck.

"You have to understand. I thought that if she—"

"Shut up," I snapped. "You don't get to speak. This is my turn. You sit there and fucking listen."

She blinked rapidly, and the hand resting on her thigh trembled.

"*My sons* have decided they want to live with me. You will not try to stop them. You will not contact them unless they contact you. But that will be their choice, not mine. I'd never be so hatefully manipulative to my children and keep them from their parent." I stood and advanced on her until I was looking down at her quaking form.

The fear in her gaze as she looked up at me was something that filled me with a sick power. No, I wasn't proud of the fact that I was scaring a woman, but she was finally getting a taste of her own medicine. The scars she left on not just me, but on our sons were unforgivable.

Loathing seeped from my pores and dripped from my words. "What you did was reprehensible. Besides ignoring the fact that they were *hawks and would need to learn to shift,* the pain you inflicted on *our children* is the cruelest thing one parent could do to the other and their innocent children. It makes you no mother at all. It makes you a hateful, selfish cunt of the first order."

With each word I said, her eyes grew wider until I thought they would burst from her head. It was as if she couldn't believe what I was saying or what I'd said wasn't what she was expecting. It set off little alarm bells that I ignored because her feelings didn't matter to me.

"I swear, I didn't want to lie to you, but Hatham was jealous of you. He hated the fact that the boys were yours. He threatened to kill you and have them sent away. I was only trying to protect them," she pleaded with tears shimmering in her brown eyes.

"You expect me to believe that?"

"It's the truth!"

Yet, I didn't believe a word she said. I huffed in contempt as I slowly shook my head.

"You disgust me. The fact that I once thought I loved you, allowed you to be the mother of my children, and gave you the power to rip my soul to shreds, makes me sick," I spat with a derisive curl of my lip. "But unfortunately, you *are* Sam and Seth's mother. And know that the only reason I'm not ripping your throat out is because of that."

"Adrien… she's an illegitimate stripper. That's who you want our boys around?"

"Since I'm feeling magnanimous, I'm going to pretend you didn't just say that. I'll also leave you with this little warning… if you fuck with my woman in any way, there won't be anywhere for you to hide. Hurt her, and I'll return it to you threefold. Understand?" I laughed darkly when her attention flickered to the tiny camera mounted in the corner of the room. "They aren't catching a thing. Everything has been bypassed—it's as if I was never here."

Her sharp inhale preceded her stuttering exhale, but I didn't stick around to interact further because I was finished with her. I padded past her in my bare feet, and I let myself out the patio door and onto the well-manicured lawn of their massive backyard. With the new moon but a dark shadow high above me, I stripped out of my clothes, rolled them tightly together, and wrapped the band around them, then released my inner hawk. Now that I'd gotten back into the rhythm of shifting, the transformation was less excruciating and the freedom of taking flight—exhilarating.

Sam and Seth were waiting, as was Sage. I had a family to get back to, and I needed to call Facet to thank him for his help with the cameras and security system in Falina's house.

My feathers ruffled in the wind, and I ate up the night sky as I soared on my way back to the clubhouse. Peace settled in my soul as I flew. With each flap of my wings, I seemed to shed some of the discontent from the past.

Now if I could figure out who had hired a hitman to kill Sage and tear him to shreds, I'd be happy.

TWO

Sage

"WALKIN' ON THE SUN"—SMASH MOUTH

Being with the President of the RBMC Dallas Chapter was at times lonely, and at others exhausting. In both a good and bad way. The sexy, gruff, bossy man that I'd been in love with since I was seventeen was intense to say the least. Yet he was my everything.

"You need anything, Sage?" Seth asked. Though he was the spitting image of his father, the teen was a quiet, slightly introverted, and kind-hearted boy. How he'd managed to maintain that inner kindness with the bitch of a mother he'd had was a minor miracle. Then again, Sam, Raptor's oldest son, had been an amazing big brother over the years. Adrien's son, I meant. I needed to train my brain to think of my sexy man as Adrien, but it was hard. I'd known him as Raptor for over ten years. Sam had kept holding their father in a good light despite the lies they'd been told. Both boys were, quite frankly, exceptional.

"Actually, if you could help me get my fat ass up off this

chair, I'd be eternally grateful." I held out a hand as I pushed myself to sitting on the lounger I'd been sprawled out on. Though still cool by Iowa standards, it was a beautifully unseasonably warm day for Texas. I'd taken advantage of it to rest as I soaked up the sun.

The scowl that pulled at his handsome face made him look so much like his father I had to fight my laughter.

"You're pregnant with my little brother or sister, not fat," he grumbled.

We had decided not to find out the sex of the little beast in my belly. I wanted the surprise—the stereotypical "It's a… *insert baby's sex!*" announcement from the doctor—and Adrien indulged me. I knew he wanted to know, but he also wanted me to be happy. It might be the only child I ever had since I wasn't sure Adrien could handle the stress of me being pregnant again—I wanted the experience to be as memorable as possible. Lordy, he was an overprotective mother hen with me.

"Yeah, well, pregnant or fat, I need help," I tossed back as I wiggled my arms in the air in a plea for help up.

The dark-haired boy chuckled and helped heave my ass up off the chair. A shiver hit me as a cool breeze blew over my exposed skin, and I grabbed the hoodie I'd shed earlier. The sun was setting and the temp was dropping.

"Holy shit," I huffed as I leaned over to rest my hands on my knees. When I pushed upright, I groaned and placed a hand on my lower back.

"We need a pool back here for the summer," Seth

observed as he stood, arms akimbo, glancing at the "backyard" behind the clubhouse.

"I second that. I'm bringing it up with your father tonight." The area of land behind the clubhouse needed a helluva lot to be called a backyard, but a pool was a great start.

A slow, satisfied grin lit his dark features. I wasn't sure if it was from my mention of discussing the pool or at my reference to Adrien as his father. It was all very new for him, but he'd been quicker to warm up to the situation. Sam was a bit more reserved and wary. Again, I sensed that was because, while he sheltered Seth from what their mother had led them to believe was the truth, he still carried the weight of abandonment on his shoulders. It was a fucked-up situation, but one Adrien worked to rectify on a daily basis.

"Come on. I'll make you an orange smoothie when we get inside," Seth offered as he gave me his elbow to use for balance as I waddled myself into the clubhouse. The boy already had my weird pregnancy craving down pat. Never in my life would I have wanted a freaking orange smoothie prior to the last several months.

"You know how to spoil a girl," I told him with a smirk that had him chuckling.

Inside the doorway, I sighed at the heavenly warmth. Seth walked with me to the stool, then went behind the bar to make my drink. The grind of the blender echoed through the clubhouse after he'd poured and dumped all the ingredients in and hit the button.

Once it was done, he poured the creamy, orangey concoction into a big glass that he set in front of me. He grabbed a straw from the container and poked it in the top. Then he washed and dried the pitcher portion before placing it back on the base.

Trying not to think about everything that had been running on a loop in my head for the past few months, I happily moaned at the first sip. I hated where my head went when I was alone.

In my defense, my life had done a complete one-eighty. I'd gone from being a stripper and club manager to being a bloated and eight-months-pregnant… nothing. I helped out at the clubhouse as best I could, and made dinner for the guys after they spent the day working on all the tiny houses Adrien had brought in. Except I had no real purpose other than being an incubator to an active little alien that thought my bladder was a trampoline and my ribs were hand and footholds.

"Good?" Seth asked as he leaned his forearms on the edge of the bar top. He'd been tasked with watching out for me today. Poor kid.

"Delicious," I corrected. "But I need to move to a table. There's not enough room on these stools for my ass right now."

He rolled his eyes but swiped the drink from me and carried it to a nearby table. I followed at my waddling pace, then unceremoniously dropped into one of the chairs. "So much better. You can go find Sam if you want. I'm not going anywhere. I'll probably go take a nap after I finish this." I motioned to the delicious drink.

"You sure?" His brow furrowed as his amber eyes flickered over my features, seeking any sign I was fibbing.

"Positive."

The way his face lit before he hugged me had my chest tightening and warm, fuzzy feelings flittering around in there. "If you need me—"

I held up a hand. "Seth, I'm a big girl. I don't need a babysitter—regardless of what your father may think."

I heard the door open and glanced over my shoulder. My shoulders dropped a bit that it was Blade and not Adrien. You'd think it had been days since I'd seen him, not mere hours.

Seth gave him a fist bump in passing.

"How are you feeling?" Blade asked as he sat beside me. Sweat dripped from his brow and he used his shirtsleeve to wipe it off. He motioned to where my hand rested on the now massive swell of my pregnant belly.

"Good," I replied with a smile that I wasn't sure reached my eyes. Adrien and I were cautiously navigating the waters of being together. Yet, he still hadn't officially made me his ol' lady, and that gave me some hesitation. Despite his blatant claim on me, he still hadn't placed his brand on me or had a cut made for me. It was bothering me more than I ever thought it would. It made me question everything. ol' lady

He'd been burned in the past, but so had I—by someone a child should've received unconditional love from.

"Don't bullshit me," he wryly shot back.

Raptor's REVENGE

"Fine. I feel fat, useless, and a little afraid," I grumbled, dropping my gaze to my hand.

He sighed. "Babe, you're beautiful, and I know Raptor tells you that daily. You're pregnant, not useless, and he's protective of you—as he should be. You don't need to be out there helping with construction. Now tell me what you're afraid of."

I cast a worried glance at the door.

"You're safe—they're finishing up the last of the sheet rock in the cabins. They'll still be a while."

"Then why are you in here?" I asked with a smirk, trying to change the subject.

"Because I was working on some things in the back with Phoenix. He ran into town to see Sloane and the little princess, so I came in here. Now, answer my question." The man was relentless.

Trying to buy time, I picked up the glass of orangey goodness in front of me and took an extra-long drink. Before I could drown myself, he took it from me and gave me a stern stare. I huffed.

"It's stupid, I know, but he hasn't mentioned giving me his brand. Not once. Sure, he calls me his ol' lady, but I have no cut and no brand. I can't help feeling like he's keeping me at a distance or maybe his family doesn't think I'm good enough for him. Hell, I'm not sure if *I* think I am," I muttered.

"Jesus H. Christ, Sage. Are you serious?" He looked at me askance. "That man is head over heels for you. He refers to you as his ol' lady in front of all the brothers. You're pregnant. He's not going to put his brand on you until after the baby is born. As far as a cut, I don't think any of the ol' ladies have them."

"There's technically only one besides me," I deadpanned.

"Still… why don't you talk to him? Tell him what your worries are."

"Because what if he tells me I'm his ol' lady but not in a… permanent way?" I muttered. All my insecurities tumbled around in my head. Despite my continuous crush on Adrien over the years, they were the reason I never wanted to get involved with a man to this extent. The power it gave men was dangerous, the potential for heartache, too great.

"Not gonna happen, but like I said, talk to him. He spent years keeping you at arm's length, but once he finally gave in, he was a goner. I've never seen the man act like he does with you. He loves you fiercely. Stop worrying—but if you can't, then just ask him."

The door flew open, and the boisterous, sweaty group of Royal Bastards barged in. Blade stood up and stared at Adrien whose eyes narrowed.

"You better not've said anything," I ground out through clenched teeth.

Blade shot me a mischievous grin, then slapped a hand over his heart like I'd physically wounded him with my accusation. "I didn't *say* a word."

Adrien made a beeline for me and stopped behind me to bury his sweat-soaked face in my neck and place his hands over mine on my bulging middle.

"Ewww! You're all sweaty!" I swatted at him and lifted my shoulder to push him away.

"You don't usually complain about that," he murmured in my ear.

"You're usually naked and we're both sweaty," I shot back.

He lifted his head and stared intently at Blade before growling, then he focused on my profile. "What the fuck, babe?"

"What?" I innocently asked as I glared at Blade's retreating back.

"Don't *what* me. How could you have any doubts about how I feel about you?" he whispered in my ear. Using his stupidly strong arms, he turned my chair so he could kneel in front of me. Unconcerned about his brothers laughing and joking at the bar not far away, he spanned my rounded stomach with his hands. Then he lifted his deep-brown gaze to mine. The little flecks of gold in them shifted and settled.

"Sage, I love you. I'm not sure how much plainer I can be. You are mine. Little junior is mine. I was a fucking idiot for leaving you behind, and I'll never be able to make up for that, but I plan to try for the rest of my life. I'm not giving you up. Ever." He pressed a kiss to the space between the edges of his splayed thumbs, and my wild-ride hormones kicked in.

With a sniffle, I mumbled, "What if it's a girl?"

"Oh Christ," he muttered under his breath and gently laid his forehead where he'd kissed. "Don't do that to me.

I seriously don't have enough guns. I'd have to call in my whole family, including Evan…. Ugh."

I softly chuckled. "Evan loves you. And he regrets the misunderstandings and circumstances that separated you two for all those years. All he wants is for you two to mend the rift and be close again."

"Has he been talking to you?" He lifted his head with a scowl, and his dark, wet hair dropped over one eye.

The corner of my mouth kicked up as I pushed it back. "No. Your mom and Reyn."

Reyn was Adrien's cousin and Evan's older sister—who was also my OB doctor. At first I was a little weirded out when his mom suggested her, but then I met her, and she was super down-to-earth and had boatloads of patience for all my questions.

I still had a hard time wrapping my head around the fact that practically his entire family was in the medical field. They were all crazy smart, and from what I gathered, very well-off. Yet you wouldn't know it by talking with them. They were just like normal, everyday people. However, it didn't stop me from feeling very inferior each time I was with them—I didn't even have a high school diploma.

"Figures," he grumbled, then sighed. "I'm trying, babe. I really am. But right now I don't give two shits about him—it's more important to me that you believe my feelings for you. The minute it's safe to do so, you'll be wearing my brand—that I can promise you."

"What if your parents find out I was a stripper?" I whispered, heart in my throat. In the short time since he'd introduced us, I'd completely and totally fallen in love with not just Sam and Seth, but Adrien's parents too. The idea of seeing their respect for me plummet made me regret every decision I'd ever made except the one to pursue him.

His gaze locked on mine, bold and steady, and he reached one hand up to grip the front of my neck. Using it to pull me closer, he brought his lips to mine. "They wouldn't care. You make me happy, I love you, you love me, and you're having my baby. That is all that would matter to them. They know your heart, and that's what's important to them."

With each word, his lips brushed mine and our breath mingled. Then he caught my lower lip in his teeth and tugged before saying, "Come with me."

Powerless to the way his words affected my body, I stood up when he did. Again, my hand went to my back, and I winced.

"Sore?" He frowned.

"Yeah. All this weight out front is doing a number on my back," I explained with a sigh.

Gently, he brushed the loose strands of my hair back, then framed my face. The little flecks of gold in his warm brown eyes seemed to glitter as he stroked my cheeks with his thumbs.

"Let me see if I can help," he murmured. He stepped back enough to reach for my hand to guide me to walk ahead of him. As we went to our room, he massaged my shoulders, and I whimpered at how amazing it felt. When I paused to open the door, he leaned forward and teased the slope of my shoulder with soft kisses.

Goose bumps broke out across my skin at the sensation. "Take a shower with me," he softly instructed as he removed my hoodie.

Unable to form words as he reached around to cup my heavy breasts, my head lolled to the side, and I moaned. He scraped his teeth along the exposed tendons of my neck, making me his willing slave. He knew that was one of my favorite things.

Without me realizing it, he had slowly worked us into the bathroom. His dark eyes found mine in the mirror as he slowly slid the thin straps of my tank top down until they hung useless over my arms. Pinching the front of the shirt, he pulled it down at an achingly slow pace, the lace at the top dragging over my peaked nipples.

I gasped at the cool air hitting them. His fingers plucked and twisted, quickly warming them up. Then he lifted the bottom of the shirt, exposing my belly. When I grunted in protest and tried to pull it back down, he stilled my hands. "You're beautiful," he murmured as we continued to stare at our reflections. "Don't hide yourself from me."

"I'm not. My hair is a mess, I don't have a lick of makeup on, my boobs are gross, and I'm huge," I argued.

He cocked a brow. "Don't you know that's when you're most beautiful to me? Nothing hiding your beauty and my child nestled safe inside you, there's not a damn thing in the world that is more stunning." His rough fingertips traced over the shadowed blue veins that now mapped my breasts. I hated them, but he made me feel like they were works of art.

My brows pinched in the center, and my chest ached as a million butterflies exploded within me. The man always knew what to say to make me feel better. There was nothing sexier than a man who appreciated his woman and worshipped her natural beauty no matter how she thought she looked. I melted.

I rested my hands over his that were still splayed over me. "I love you," I told him as I held his intense gaze.

The corner of his mouth kicked up, and he slowly spun me to face him. With his middle finger softly stroking my lower lip, he grinned. "And I fucking love you."

Reverently, he undressed me and turned on the water. When he was sure the temperature was right, he helped me in. With sure hands and deft fingers, he washed my hair and soaped my body. Slowly, he smoothed his palms down my arms until our fingers laced, and he pressed my hands to the wall. "Don't move them," he whispered in my ear in a way that told me it was an order.

Using the slick foam, he massaged my lower back, then up my spine to my shoulders before repeating it several more times. His touch was brilliant magic, and I dropped my head because holding it up required too much effort. One by one, my muscles unknotted and relaxed.

"I've wanted you since you were too young for me and my tastes. With each year that passed, it was harder and harder to resist you. Especially when you kept fucking with me. Pushing. Every. Button." He punctuated that with deep swirling digs into the muscles of my now languid body. "I didn't care that you slept with other men. It was your choice and your right to do anything and everything that made you feel good. But I knew I'd never be able to share you, so I wasn't going to stifle you. Finally, I couldn't do it anymore. Couldn't fight it anymore."

A groan escaped me as he hit a particularly sore spot, and he slid his thick cock through the slippery crack of my ass.

"You can't make those sounds, baby. Look what you do to me." He stroked it through again, and I clawed at the shower tiles—because I was literally climbing the walls to get him to drive inside. "I hate that it took me so long to give in, because you're perfect for me in every way."

As he rinsed the suds away, his mouth followed. He licked and sucked, kissed and nibbled until I was panting with my need for him—each exhale a little whimper.

"Adrien," I begged. But instead of giving me what I wanted, he quickly washed himself, then turned off the water and reached for the towels he'd placed on the sink. Inch by inch, he dried me, then lifted me into his arms, causing me to squeak in surprise.

With ease, he carried me out of the bathroom. He sat me on the edge of the bed, then nudged my legs apart. When I reached for his jutting cock, he gave a sharp inhale. My mouth watered as I leaned forward to bring the silky-soft head between my parted lips.

"Fuck," he hissed. Except instead of letting me continue, he pressed on my shoulders to tell me he wanted me to lie back. "Not yet."

I pouted and huffed, but he just chuckled darkly. He

trailed his hands over what seemed like every inch of me before going to his knees and resting my parted legs over his hard, muscular shoulders.

When his short beard teased along my inner thighs, I gasped, and my fingers found his messy wet hair. Like the devil he was, he tortured me by running his hot tongue everywhere but where I wanted it most. When he plunged it into my slit then inside me, I clenched around his tongue and groaned because he was almost there. Still, he got close but never close enough. What started as a sensual kiss to my aching pussy grew needy until he attacked me—wild and without restraint.

"Fucking gorgeous," he growled before he bit my clit, and I cried out. Unfortunately, he didn't stay there. "The most stunning creature I've ever seen."

I fisted his hair and tugged, trying like hell to get him where I wanted him, but it was hard because I was reaching around my stomach. I lifted my hips, trying to grind into his face, but he held me in place. "Goddammit, Adrien!"

He chuckled darkly as he made a slow swipe from my ass to my clit but never stayed long enough in one spot. I was thrashing in desperation—which was exactly how he wanted me. When a sob escaped me, he finally had mercy and sucked hard on my engorged clit. Slowly, he slipped two fingers in to curl against the spot only he had ever been able to find so quickly and so goddamn magically.

I shattered—a million pieces cast into the atmosphere. Pulsing bliss was my new existence, and I never wanted to go back to reality. Except all good things must end, and slowly, my vision cleared and I drifted back to earth. Panting, I lay there, boneless and replete.

Until he moved up and braced on his arms above me. A wicked grin curved his lips—the glisten of my release painted on them. When he lowered himself to kiss me, I not only tasted myself on his tongue, I felt the silken skin of his thick cock pressed on my stomach.

Torn between needing him inside me and wanting to taste him, I moaned. Then I pushed him back. "Help me up," I insisted, feeling completely huge and as unsexy as a person could be.

His brows drew in, and he canted his head but did as I said. Before he could stop me, I dropped to my knees at his feet and took his length into my mouth. I'd never been more thankful for the memory-foam rug I'd had the good sense to buy for just such an occasion. He palmed his face with both hands and sucked in a sharp breath. "Fuuuuuck" was his exhale.

He gathered my hair in his hand and tugged enough to get my attention. Thick cock still filling my mouth, I looked up at him.

"Fucking beautiful." He slowly slid deeper, and I maintained eye contact as I cupped his ass in my splayed hands. "Jesus."

Then I showed him Jesus, all right.

By the time I had swallowed every drop of his cum, he was practically cross-eyed, and his knees were buckling. He fell sideways onto the bed as I awkwardly crawled up next to him. He wrapped his arm around me and tucked me into his big spoon, then protectively cradled our now kicking-like-hell baby.

"Fuckin' love you," he mumbled into my tangled hair.

"Mmm, love you too," I returned as I wiggled my ass against him in an attempt to get closer. He let go of me long enough to grab the blanket I had folded at the foot of the bed and tossed it over us.

Like this, everything was right with the world, and together, we were invincible.

But as I drifted into my well-deserved nap, an insidious feeling washed over me. And though we were insulated in our little cocoon of bliss, the cloud of my past hung dark and heavy above me.

It was like waiting for the other shoe to drop.

THREE

Raptor

"NIGHTMARE"—SET IT OFF

"Hey, Prez, there's something I need you to see," Ares called out from the doorway of my small office where I was in the process of paying bills. I fucking hated office work, but One Short, who was our secretary/treasurer, had to go out of town unexpectedly because his dad fell and broke his hip. The frown on Ares's face had me jumping up and following him out to the UTV. We went off toward the east side of the property and followed the fence line.

"Imminent danger?" I asked him, wondering if we needed backup.

"No. At least I didn't see anything on my way back."

I nodded.

After a fairly bumpy ride, he cut the motor. We climbed out, and he made his way over to a spot where the cedars were growing along and through the high fence. He pushed the branches to the side and pointed to what appeared to be fresh tracks and a spot where the fence was cut.

"What the fuck?" I asked as I stood upright and squinted, my gaze traveling over the land. Nothing else seemed amiss, but why would someone come through here? "Did they get into the shed or the pit in the back?"

"That was my first thought, but no. The tracks go toward the compound before they disappear. I couldn't find anything up there that was messed with—at least nothing evident." Ares also glanced around. I got what he was thinking, because I felt suddenly exposed.

"Have you shown Gator?" I asked him.

"No, I went directly to you as soon as I found it," he replied. "I'll get it fixed, but I wanted you to see it first."

"No. Leave it. I don't want them knowing we found it."

He frowned as he tilted his head.

"I want you to see if we can get some surveillance set up out here. We need to know who it is and what they're doing. If we let them know we're onto them, they'll find a different route, and it may be one we won't see coming," I explained. Fucking hell, I hated this shit. It was always something.

"Understood."

Ares and I got in the UTV and headed back to the compound, stopping outside the cabin everyone was working on today. We went inside, and the boys all stopped what they were doing when they saw us.

"What's up, boss man?" Gator asked as he lifted the safety goggles onto his forehead and set his nail gun down.

We filled them in on what Ares had found. No one was happy.

"I'll get my guy in and set up a camera," Gator offered. "He's discreet and I trust him, but it would be nice if we had a tech guy of our own. What's the word with that spec-ops guy that you know, Torque?"

"He's finishing up his paperwork to get out, and then he'll be here. I talked to him on Friday, and he said he's thinking he'll be here by the end of the month." Torque had gone to high school with the guy, and over the years, they'd kept in touch. He was looking at coming back to the Dallas area and opening a home-security company or some shit. Torque had been talking to him about hanging out with us and possibly joining the club.

"What about Sage?" Blade asked with a cocked brow.

I blew out a heavy breath as I scrubbed my hands down my face. Then I stared into his gaze with heavy resignation. "I was hoping it was only me who was afraid this had anything to do with her. That maybe I was overreacting. You know?"

"Bro, you're not a fucking idiot. If you thought it, there was some credence to it. Besides, there's a reason you don't let her go anywhere alone. We all know this isn't finished. So if suddenly we have some fucker coming onto the property, the logical conclusion would be that it had something to do with her." Blade shook his head.

"Blade is right. We never found out who hired that fucker who's now incinerated in the pit. If he was following her here, we have to assume he communicated with whoever hired him and that they know she's here," Gator said, sagely voicing the worries that had been swirling in my head since we caught that guy. He studied my reaction to his observation.

"Trust me, I get it. What I don't get is why someone would be so fixated on killing her that they would chase her all the way to Texas." I met the concerned gazes of my brothers. "I'd appreciate it if she wasn't made aware of our concerns. She doesn't need the added stress during her pregnancy. As far as she's concerned, she will simply have escorts because I'm an overprotective fucker."

"Prez, with all due respect, I think you might want to give her a heads-up. She's your woman and having your kid. You have a right to make sure she's safe, but she needs to be aware and pay attention to her surroundings," Torque hesitantly inserted.

"She's my ol' lady," I corrected.

"Oh, sorry, yeah. I meant she's your ol' lady." He looked appropriately sheepish at his error.

I didn't hold it against him, but in that brief interaction, I understood where Sage was coming from a bit better. I'd never been one to give a shit about what anyone else thought. I figured I knew where my feelings and intentions with Sage were at, and that was that. Obviously, Sage wasn't as certain, and my brothers must not be clear either. Not if in their mind she was designated as the woman carrying my child and not my ol' lady.

"We don't have any prospects to put on that task, and we need every pair of hands we can get to finish the cabins. My family has offered to help if we ever need them. I'll reach out to them. I'd appreciate you all keeping an eye out too. Watch for anything out of the ordinary and basically stay on your toes." I sighed in frustration because I hated to be indebted to anyone—family or not.

My next order of affairs was to take care of ensuring my woman had some clarification.

"Not a problem," Phoenix confirmed. "She's our president's ol' lady, and she's pregnant with his child, but more than that is the fact that we all love her too."

Though I know he didn't mean it like that, a possessive feeling burned through me that screamed, "She's mine!" I shook it off, but it still simmered.

"By the way, Phoenix, I need a minute." I motioned him to follow me outside, leaving Ares inside to help the guys with the finishing touches on the cabin. We were making fast work of getting them completed, and I was hoping to have everyone moved in before Christmas. At least for those who wanted to stay on-site.

Phoenix followed me outside to where I waited on the small front porch.

"Yeah?" He canted his head with a questioning frown.

"Your brother reached out to me. He wanted to talk about becoming a hangaround for the club." No sense in beating around the bush. Phoenix was either going to be okay with it or not. If he wasn't, then I'd tell Keenan no.

He blew out a heavy breath and hung his head. Hands on

his hips, shoulders slumped, he lifted his gaze to mine. "Yeah. He asked me about it. I told him to stop by and talk to you."

"How do you feel about that?"

"Fuck, I don't know."

"So, do you want me to tell him no?"

"No, I actually don't. Does it make sense that I'm not even sure why we're mad anymore?" Phoenix stared across the property, appearing lost in thought for a moment. "I've reached that point where I feel like we wasted so many years."

His words sent a pang through my chest that I tried to inconspicuously rub out. It was a little too close to home with me and my family—especially Evan. Crazy how it took Phoenix's observation of his relationship with his brother to make me clearly see where I was sitting. Falina had proven to me that she was vindictive, selfish, and untruthful. Yet, here I was, holding my cousin accountable for 100 percent of the situation and not letting him explain his side of things.

"Yeah, I totally get it," I replied as I swallowed hard and covered it by clearing my throat. "We'll bring it to the table and put it to the vote, but I don't see an issue."

Phoenix pulled out a pack of cigarettes.

"I thought you quit?" I asked with a smirk.

He lit one with the spark that appeared when he rubbed his thumb over his fingertips, then took a long drag. "I did."

I cocked a brow.

"Don't fucking judge me, man. Brigit hasn't been sleeping the past couple of nights and is fussy as fuck. Sloane thinks she's teething. Just you wait. You'll be dealing with this shit too," he grumbled.

And another realization hit me that had me questioning myself and everything in my life. I was in my midthirties and getting ready to be a father again. I'd be in my fifties when my kid graduated high school. I was almost ten years older than Sage. Fucking hell, I'd never felt so old in my goddamn life.

"Better not let Sloane find out," I warned with a good-natured grin.

"Hmpf!" He rolled his eyes while inhaling deeply again. "So, what's up with Blade?"

"What do you mean?"

"I mean, he brought your woman down here, and he hasn't left yet. He staying or what?"

"He hasn't put in for a transfer, so I couldn't say. Ask him yourself," I replied. I wasn't sure what Blade's plans were. Last time we had discussed it, he had shrugged and told me he hadn't decided. Like I'd said before, I'd love to have him, but that was his decision.

"Hmm. Okay, well, if you don't need anything else, I'm gonna get back to work."

I nodded. "No, that was it. Now I need to track down my woman and check on her. And let her know I'm going to have someone watching her every time she leaves the compound. She's gonna love that. I'll come back out to help after I finish up with the accounting bullshit and talk to her."

One Short couldn't get back soon enough.

Striding across the open area between the cabins and the clubhouse, I paused. A chill skated down my spine. Sending my inner hawk out, I scanned the area, but I didn't come up with anything that could've set my senses off like that.

Great. Now I'm being paranoid.

Inside, I found Sage with the boys at the table, playing dominos. They all glanced at the door when it opened. Curious stares turned to smiles as their faces lit up when they saw it was me.

"Hello, handsome," Sage purred. Though she had shed the platinum-blonde hair when she and Blade fled Iowa and she was now hugely pregnant, she still was the quintessential pinup girl in my book. No makeup or her face fully done, dressed up or down—she was stunning. Thick lashes framed her sky-colored eyes that said the things she couldn't with the boys present. I smirked.

"Need to talk to you, babe. It won't take long," I clarified.

"Snack break!" Seth called out and the boys both scrambled from their chairs and rushed to the kitchen. Sage and I both chuckled.

I held out my hand, and she placed hers in mine so I could help her up. "This is ridiculous," she muttered and dropped her gaze. "I can't even see my damn feet."

"Well, if it's any consolation, they're still there, and they look as cute as the rest of you."

She wiggled her bright-red painted toes. With her rounded belly pressing into me, she looped her arms around my neck and her mouth curved. "I'm cute, huh?"

My hands found her hips, and I firmly gripped them. "Actually, no." Her plush lips fell open and her eyes went wide. "You're fucking beautiful."

A soft pink bloomed on her cheeks, and her eyes glistened. Lifting one arm, I hooked my hand around the side of her neck. Using my thumb, I gently swept over the soft skin along her jawline.

"For someone who was so damn gruff and grumpy for years, you sure know the right things to say."

Laughter huffed out of me. "Come on."

She trailed behind me as I kept a hold on her by twining my fingers with hers. We went into our room, and I closed the door. Spinning, I took her other hand and held them both over her head.

"Mmm, I thought you said it wouldn't take long," she teased with a twinkle in her eyes as she blinked up at me.

"Baby, I could make you and me both come in five minutes flat, but that's not what I asked you in here for," I told her. A crooked smile lifted one side of my lips.

"Promises, promises," she whispered, and my cock came to life.

I growled, which only gave her a wicked gleam in those mesmerizing baby blues.

"I'm going to have someone watching over you," I announced, and her eyes narrowed.

"You mean, I'm gonna have a babysitter."

"No, more like a bodyguard." I sighed in frustration because I really didn't want to ruin her mood, yet Torque was right—I needed to give her a heads-up. "We still don't know who hired the guy to follow you. I'm not willing to risk you or the baby's safety. I thought about not telling you because I didn't want you to worry, but the guys thought you needed to be informed so you can remain vigilant."

Her face softened. "Baby, I'm not a fragile flower, and I'm not stupid."

"I know you're not, but I worry about you."

With my thumbs, I caressed the silky insides of her forearms that I still held against the door above her head. "You sure you don't have that five minutes?" she asked in a breathy whisper.

In answer, I leaned down and sank my teeth into the muscles on her arched neck. I licked and sucked my way up and along her jaw. The sweet sigh that slipped out before she drew her lower lip between her teeth gave me a full-on stiffy. As I teased the seam of her mouth with my tongue, I pushed it into her hip so she could see how bad I wanted her.

"Five minutes," I finally conceded. "Bend over, hands on the dresser."

The second I released her hands, she did as she was told. As our gazes locked, I curled my fingers around the front of her throat. Her pulse pounded against my fingers and her eyes darkened.

"God, I want to play, but I don't have time."

"Then fuck me," she boldly suggested.

Smoothing my hand down her lush body, I found her fuzzy sleeping pants and ripped them down to expose her ass. The entire time, we stared at each other's reflections. My palm connected to her smoothly rounded globe with a crack, and she sucked in a startled breath. I repeated the action against the other one, then dipped my hand between her legs.

"Dripping," I observed with satisfaction as I slipped a finger under the tiny panel that covered her pussy. I hooked the crotch and tugged them down to join her pants around her ankles. Then I freed my cock and stroked it before I lined it up.

Feeding the head in, I reveled in her slippery heat that stretched around me. I made short strokes inside that deepened each time I drove my hips forward. With as wet as she was, it wasn't long before I was seated to the base.

By then, both of us were practically panting, and we hadn't even started yet. "Fuck me, Adrien," she begged.

Not one to disappoint my girl, I pulled almost all the way out before I thrust hard. With each stroke I pulled her hips hard back against mine. Her eyes practically rolled as I did exactly what she wanted and fucked the living hell out of her.

Once I could feel my balls draw up and my spine got that familiar tingle, I reached around and under her stomach to flick and circle her swollen clit. That elicited a throaty moan, and I pinched it. "Come on my cock, goddammit."

Ever my obedient girl, she did exactly as I asked. The almost violent spasms of her tight cunt around my shaft set me off, and I filled her pussy with my cum.

A quick peek at my watch had me grinning. "Four and a half minutes."

The burst of bright laughter made my heart damn near explode. I loved her so fucking much, I couldn't see straight at times. Holding myself deep in her body, I told her, "I fucking love you."

"Yeah?"

"Yeah."

"Mmm, well, that's good, because I fucking love you too." Our shared laughter had me starting to slip out.

"I have something for you."

"Oh, do you?" One narrow brow arched as she tried to hold back her smile.

Regretfully, I withdrew, but not without holding her ass cheeks open to watch. A deep satisfaction heated my blood at the sight of our mixed release following me out. I wanted to take it and paint her body in it. God, I was a caveman. Instead, I went into the bathroom and snagged a towel that I tossed to her.

Then, I went into the closet and grabbed the flat box I had placed on the top shelf, knowing she couldn't reach it. By the time I turned around, she had cleaned up and fixed her clothing. She sat happily with her legs in that pretzel-ass way that only women seemed to be able to do. Though I didn't mess up her hair that was loosely piled on her head, she still looked thoroughly fucked. She was gorgeous.

"I was going to give you this after junior was born, but I think you need it now." I handed it to her, and she took it from me with a curious tilt of her head.

When she opened it and pushed the tissue back, she gasped. With one hand over her mouth and tears in her eyes, she sniffled. "Adrien," she whispered as she reached in and lifted the soft, supple black leather.

The patch on the back of the cut read "RBOL" with another below it that said "Property of Raptor."

"I don't want you getting my mark while you're pregnant, but you can bet your sweet ass that once Reyn gives the okay, I'm taking you down to get inked." Gently, I cupped her jaw and lifted her chin with my thumb. Her glistening blue eyes took my breath away as she stared up at me. "You and my children are the most important people in my life—you're my *world*. I would do anything for you. If I lost you, *I'd* be lost. I'm not sure what else I can do to prove to you that you're it for me, baby."

With tears spilling over and trailing down her cheeks, she swallowed hard.

"My whole life I've fought the little voice inside that says I'm not worthy. Becoming Cookie allowed me to take control of my life and my body. It let me push that nagging voice away and pretend that I wasn't Sage, the little broken girl. Maybe a lot of my feelings of vulnerability lately stem from that. As Cookie, I was the woman I wanted to be. Moving down here and taking my name back rocked my foundation a little more than I realized. I know it causes problems for me and it makes me an insecure pain in the ass. I'm sorry for that." She hugged the leather vest to her chest like a security blanket.

"You don't need to be sorry," I counter.

"But I am. Because of my worries, I've made you feel like you have something to prove. That was what I expected when I first got down here, but not now." She smirked, and the corners of my mouth tipped up.

"It took me a minute to get my shit together, but the moment I saw you, I knew I had messed up. Thinking you were here as Blade's girl sent me into a jealous rage, and I took it out on you. Which was asinine because I'd been the chickenshit who had left you behind. The way you made me feel terrified me because I'd sworn to never trust a woman again. My point is, neither of us is perfect, but I never want you to question my dedication or loyalty to you. I love you, and you. Are. Mine." I rested my hand on the large curve of her belly. "And little junior here is mine. That is never going to change."

"Juniorette," she corrected, and we both laughed.

"I have some shit to take care of, and I'm sure the boys are wondering what the hell we're doing," I muttered, reluctant to leave her. No matter how much I wanted to say fuck it and take her back to bed, I needed to reach out to my family. I needed their help again.

"They aren't babies, Adrien. I bet they know exactly what we were doing." A light pink flush colored her cheeks, but she still grinned ear to ear.

"Well, come on, then, sexy. Let me help you up." I held out my hand.

She rested hers in mine and allowed me to assist her out of the bed. Once she was on her feet, instead of releasing me, she squeezed. "I love you too."

I dipped my head and brushed my lips over hers.

Before I could rip her clothes off and keep her captive in bed, I pulled away. "Come on, my little temptress."

I swatted her ass as she moved toward the door.

"Oh, you're gonna pay for that later," she warned.

"You like it, and you know it," I shot back.

As she rushed down the hall, she called back to me.

"Of course I do!"

FOUR

Sage

"SANTA BABY"—EARTHA KITT

"I think we should get these for the clubhouse," Niara said with a grin as she held a little mistletoe bundle in the air. Her brows waggled comically.

"You just want to hang one over your head while you're there," Sloane teased. "Especially when Blade is around."

"Umm, duh," Niara returned. The feisty redhead looked at us like we were total buzzkills.

I made a gagging motion by sticking my finger in my mouth. "Gross."

"Hey, just because he's like your brother doesn't mean he has to be mine." Niara winked, and Sloane and I laughed.

The fact that they wanted me around was still crazy. Back in Iowa, I always got along with the ol' ladies, but they didn't invite me to hang out with them. There was an unspoken line that wouldn't get crossed. I'm sure a lot of it had to do with the fact that before they got with their ol' ladies, I had fucked a lot of the club members. I had scruples though. Once they were taken, they were off my radar.

Sloane knew that I'd been with Phoenix in the past, but she welcomed me with open arms. She was like that though—loving and kind. Then by extension, I got Niara too.

Neither of them celebrated Christmas, but they had come to the Christmas Bazaar with me because they were awesome women. Honestly, I didn't know what I believed in, but Christmas or Yule was the best time of the year for me. Not for the presents or anything, but simply because I loved to decorate.

"You think I should put up a tree at the clubhouse?" I asked as I touched a finger to a handmade ornament, making the bell tinkle.

"Hey, since we celebrate Yule, we're all about the tree. Girl, that's our jam. If you want to put one up, we'll totally help you decorate it." Sloane's eyes were bright, and she clapped her hands together.

"Yeah?" I asked with a big smile.

"Of course!" Niara seconded.

"We need tons of garland too," Sloane added.

"And lights," I chimed in. A small Braxton Hicks contraction hit me. I pretty much ignored it because I'd already rushed to the hospital twice only to be told it was false labor and that the tightening of my abdomen was Braxton Hicks contractions.

"Definitely lights," both women agreed in unison.

A strange chill skated down my spine, and I glanced around to see what could've caused it, but all I saw were other shoppers and vendors. I shook it off as my imagination because of everything that I'd been through.

"That's a beautiful choice," a woman said next to me as I held up a handmade glittering crystal star for the top of the tree. Unsure if she was talking to me, I glanced over. She held two similar stars in her hands as if she was trying to decide which to get.

"Those are nice too," I offered with a smile, my hand falling to my lightly clenching stomach.

"I'm just not sure if I like the silver accents or the gold," she pondered and cocked her head as she continued to study them.

"Well, do you have tinsel or garland for your tree?" I asked.

"Hmm, I'll probably use garland, this year."

"Silver or gold?"

"Blue," she replied with a laugh that I returned.

"I'd go with the silver," Niara chimed in from over my shoulder.

"You think?" She turned to face us.

"Yep," Sloane confirmed.

The woman handed the ornament to the lady at the booth. "I'll take this one, please."

"Good choice," I told her with a grin.

"Well, thanks for your help," she returned with a brilliant smile. Then as if she had just noticed my ginormous belly, she motioned to it. "How far along are you?"

"Almost full term," I replied as she completed her purchase and I started mine.

"Your husband must be getting excited."

Her reference to Adrien as my husband quickly sobered me because that was another thing that bothered me. Despite gifting me the cut and saying I would get his mark after the birth of the baby, he hadn't made any references to us getting married in months. Instead of admitting I wasn't married, I just smiled and left the observation unconfirmed.

"Well, thanks for your help," the woman offered with a smile that seemed a bit sad before disappearing into the crowd.

My interaction with the woman left me in my head for the rest of our shopping expedition.

We bought so much that we ended up making three trips to the SUV Adrien let us borrow. It looked like a holiday-decor factory had exploded back there.

The lone hawk sitting at the top of a light pole near the vehicle gave me comfort. Malachi ruffled his feathers and settled again.

I smiled but rested a hand on the giant basketball I had under my shirt. This kid seemed like it was gaining five pounds a day. It actually felt like I had a bowling ball sitting in my lower pelvis. There was so much pressure, and it was so freaking heavy. Reyn and all the books I'd read told me to expect that the baby would "drop" as I got closer, but holy hell.

"Everything all right?" Sloane asked as she paused with her hand on the backseat door handle.

"I'm just so damn uncomfortable," I grumbled as another contraction hit me.

"Well, get in the passenger seat. I'm driving," Niara

insisted. Unwilling but not having the energy to argue, I did as she said.

The moment we left the parking spot, my stomach muscles tightened and kept getting tighter. "Oh!"

"What?" Niara practically shrieked as she glanced my way.

"I think that was a contraction," I moaned as it eased.

"You think we should stop by the hospital?" Niara asked, wide-eyed and white-knuckled.

"Don't mind her—she absolutely lost her shit when I went into labor with Brigit," Sloane teased. She asked me a bunch of questions that I answered to the best of my ability as the tightening of my abdominal muscles continued. "I think they are just Braxton Hicks, but it wouldn't hurt to swing by and get you checked out."

"Call Raptor," Niara demanded as she looked in the rearview mirror, then back at the road.

"I don't want to worry him," I argued, but her lips were pressed flat, and she seemed really serious about it.

"Call him. Now." Her tone made me frown. As did the turn she just took. We weren't going the right way. Another contraction hit me.

My phone was connected to the vehicle's Bluetooth, so I dialed his number.

"Hey, babe. How was your day with the girls?" His voice rang out through the speakers and sent warmth flooding through me.

"Good," I panted.

"Sage?" He automatically picked up on my strained reply, and I could hear the instant worry in his tone.

"Raptor, how many guys do you have on us?" Niara cut in.

"Malachi is solo, but I can make a call and head to you myself as well. What's going on? Where are you?"

Niara rattled off our location and the direction we were heading. "I have a black car that's been following us since we left the craft festival. At first I thought it was coincidence, but it has taken every turn I've made."

"Can you see Malachi?" he demanded. My heart was now pounding, and my contractions weren't stopping. Fear skated up my spine.

Sloane leaned back and forth as she looked up, and so did I—at least as best as I could. The hawk flying above gave me a little comfort. Just not enough to make my stomach stop clenching up.

"He's up there," Sloane called out.

"I'm pulling you up on my app now. I'll make a call, and we'll be there soon. Don't panic, and stay in populated areas," he insisted.

"Um, Raptor?" Sloane hesitantly asked.

"Yeah?"

"Sage is having contractions."

I glared at her, but the little imp only stuck her tongue out at me.

"Go to the hospital. Now," he insisted—like I knew he would.

"Adrien, I'm fine. It's a few of those Braxton Hicks

things," I explained in an attempt to settle him. They were easing off, anyway.

He drilled me on their timing, how I felt, how long they lasted, and a million other things.

"Traffic is backing up, Raptor. We need to find an alternate route," Niara announced.

"Shit," he muttered, and I could hear him rustling around, probably looking at the location app and getting his shit together. If he was shifting, then he was getting naked. I liked that image. "Take the second right," he told Niara. "Follow it down five blocks."

"On it," she assured him as we slowed to a near crawl and squeezed into the right-hand lane.

"Will you be okay for a few minutes? I need to reach out to my family. I'll watch you on the app, and I'll call you back."

"We'll be okay. I'm going to try to keep moving," Niara replied as she took the turn he indicated.

"Roger that. Babe?"

"Yes?"

"I fucking love you. I'll be there soon."

Despite the gravity of our current situation, I chuckled. "I love you too."

The call ended, and silence ensued. Sloane and I kept looking over our shoulder, and Niara took quick peeks in the rearview. We kept driving and following the directions Sloane had pulled up on her phone.

"They're still three cars back," I announced, though it was highly uncomfortable to twist in my seat to look back there.

"Take a left at the light," Sloane told Niara. When we

turned, the car followed, and my heart raced with my soaring anxiety. Flashbacks of the night I was run off the road slammed into me, and I clutched my chest against the rising panic.

Niara reached over and gripped my free hand. "It's going to be okay. Malachi is still with us, and Raptor will be on the way."

The phone rang, and she hit the button on the steering wheel. "We're about five blocks from the hospital," she told him without wasting time to say hello.

"Good. I'm on my way. Hang in there, Sage, I'll be with you soon."

Another contraction started to build. "Okay. Love you."

"Love you too." The call ended, and I took a stuttering breath as I squeezed my eyes shut. The way the contractions were increasing in strength told me that it might be the real thing.

"We're almost there," Niara said to soothe me.

"Okay," I gasped. The pressure was incredible. It was like my entire abdomen was in a vise. When Niara made the turn to follow the signs for the ER, I froze. "I think my water just broke."

Sloane leaned up into the front seat to look. Her brows raised, she swiveled her head to look at me. "That would be a yes. Unless your bladder is the size of a soccer ball."

"The seat!" I cried.

"Who gives a shit about the seat?" Niara shouted.

Sloane clambered out of the backseat and helped me get down from the SUV. I saw the hawk land on top of a tree that was near the ER entrance. He was watchful and scanning the area. Niara left the vehicle with the door wide open and ran inside. She immediately ran back out, pushing a wheelchair.

"Sit!" she ordered. Sloane helped me get into the chair and spun me around, then pushed me through the doors. Niara went to park the SUV. The rest was a blur, as I was too busy doubling over. I vaguely caught the receptionist telling them to take me directly to Labor and Delivery because of how far along I was.

"Why does this seem to be happening so fast?" I moaned once I could breathe again as they rolled me to the elevator.

"Girl, I hate to tell you this, but this can go on for a long damn time with your first child," Sloane replied with a wince.

"Where's Adrien?" Despite Sloane's explanation, I was beginning to panic. I needed him with me. My water breaking made this very real—the increased intensity of the contractions hammered that fact home.

"He's on his way. Probably not far now. Advantages of being able to take a direct route and avoid traffic. Right?" Sloane assured me.

"Yeah," I absently murmured. The elevator doors opened, and we were on the move again. We stopped at the desk, and one of the nurses set me up in a triage room. It didn't take long for someone to check me and have me fill out their forms. I was dilated and effaced far enough that they admitted me. In what seemed like a flurry of organized activity, I was brought to my room, gowned up, had an elastic belt monitor thingy wrapped around me, and a hospital band placed around my wrist.

"Good heavens, Adrien called me, freaking out. Men!" Reyn said as she entered the room. She held my hand when she stopped by the bedside. "Okay, Sage, are you ready for this?"

"No!" That single word was full of my dismay, and I clutched her hand like it was my lifeline. "I don't understand how my contractions seemed to get so wicked so quickly."

"My guess is, you were having contractions all day, but they were bearable, and you ignored them. There's nothing wrong with that. Once your water broke, your body realized it was showtime. Now, here we are. My question was probably not the best, since it was pretty rhetorical." Reyn cast an empathetic smile at me. "I'll be back in to check on you," she assured me, and then she left the room.

Sloane stayed by my side, but I lost track of time as the contractions wreaked havoc on my body.

"This kid is a savage," I gasped at a particularly vicious contraction. "God, where is its father?"

"I don't know, sweetheart, but I'm sure he's on his way," she offered soothingly as she gave me a spoonful of crushed ice.

There was a commotion out in the hallway, and then the man of the hour came barging into the room, eyes wild and hair disheveled. "Sage," he breathed.

Glancing down, I noticed he had a pair of HEYDUDEs on his feet that normally would've been bare after shifting.

"Reyn helped me out," he explained in answer to my wordless question.

I gave him a tight smile because another contraction was barreling down on me.

"Fuck, fuck, fuck," I chanted through gritted teeth as I curled forward. I clutched the bed rails, and tried to breathe through the contraction like I'd been taught at the handful of classes I'd gone to. It wasn't going too well.

Adrien immediately moved to my side and placed a cool rag on the back of my neck that he followed with a kiss to my sweat-soaked temple. I whimpered as my body contorted with a mind of its own.

When it started to ease, I sobbed in relief, then fell back onto my pillow.

"This child is gonna kill me," I mumbled.

"No, it isn't. You're progressing like you should, but unfortunately, it sometimes takes time. You're doing great, Sage," Reyn encouraged. She left her position of power from between my legs and pulled off her gloves.

"Great? I still have a baby in my uterus! That's not great. Great would be me holding him or her. This is not great," I grumbled as I tried to rest before the next one hit.

"Call me if you need me. I have some new moms I need to make rounds on," she told us, then left the room.

"I need her."

"For what?"

"To get this baby out right now."

FIVE

Raptor

"LIVING IN A DREAM"—FINGER ELEVEN

"L ike this?" Seth asked as I watched him line the saw up on the wood. I gave him an encouraging nod after double-checking to ensure there was no safety measure that he'd missed.

Both boys were all in with helping me get the small house finished. I was thankful I'd bought the one with a full height second-story loft. They would have to share the area until I was able to build my actual house. By then, Sam would probably be off to college, but I hoped he'd come home often to stay. He'd already been accepted to Texas A&M and planned to transfer to Baylor College of Medicine to become a doctor.

Ironic, considering he didn't really know or remember my side of the family. Then again, it wouldn't take a genius to track down my family and find out that the majority of them were in medicine. And I was pretty sure Sam was a damn genius.

Once Seth finished his task, he lifted the goggles onto the top of his head, and his grin was contagious. "That was so awesome."

I chuckled. "Well, come on, Bob the Builder, we need to get the trim finished." We were putting the final touches on the tiny house. I wanted to have it done before the baby was born. And I was tired of the boys sleeping on the pull-out couch in the clubhouse. It still baffled me that they were so adamant that they live with me, but I couldn't have been happier. I just didn't want to disappoint them—they'd had enough of that in their lives.

My phone rang, and since it was Sage's ringtone, I pulled it out. Sam and Seth snickered at the song choice. It was "Porn Star Dancing" by My Darkest Days.

I couldn't keep the grin off my face when I answered. "Hey, babe. How was your day with the girls?"

It was immediately apparent that something was wrong. After they explained what was going on, I was furious. First because someone was following them, but then because she was in *labor* and being followed by someone.

After ensuring I had her on the app we used, I made a few rushed calls, then asked the boys to hold down the fort until I could get one of the brothers to give them a ride.

"We're going with you," Sam insisted.

My brow pinched between my eyes because this would be the first time Seth would shift and make a significant flight. We were a ways from the hospital.

"I can make it," Seth eagerly assured me.

Scrubbing my hand over my mouth, I hesitated. I was wasting precious time. Then I knew I needed to get my ass in gear, and I didn't trust them not to try to follow me. They were too much like I was at their age.

"Fine, but you won't have shoes." We were going to a hospital, and they needed to be prepared. No one wanted to walk around barefoot there.

"I actually have something for that. I've been working on it since Sam first told me what was happening to him." Seth excitedly ran back to the clubhouse.

"We might as well follow him. I need to move. Now."

Seth met us out back, and he had a small pouch in his hand. He pulled a pair of HEYDUDEs, a T-shirt, a pair of boxer briefs, and a pair of lightweight khakis from it.

"Jesus. How did you fit that in there? Never mind. We need to leave."

Seth tossed a matching pouch to Sam. Reyn was already en route to the hospital because she was going in to check on some postpartum moms she had. She had a pair of her husband's shoes in the car that she said should fit me.

We all stripped down, used to being nude in front of each other by then. As one, we crouched and braced for the transition that blasted us apart at a cellular level. I could feel the almost electric ripple that waved over my skin that

I knew would be followed by our skin darkening and then morphing to feathers. I was proud and impressed with how fluidly both boys shifted now.

Our screeches filled the air, and with our compacted clothes rolled up and clutched in our taloned feet, we took flight. By air, we could take a more direct route, but it was still going to be taxing for Seth.

He surprised me, though.

"*You doing okay?*" I asked him with the telepathy we had when in hawk form.

"*Piece of cake,*" he shot back.

Another hawk joined us, and Drago chuckled. "*Well, hello, boys.*"

The four of us landed on the hospital grounds in an area I'd scoped out in advance for a situation like this. Behind the privacy fence that surrounded a bunch of pumps and electrical crap, we quickly shifted and dressed. My pride in the boys grew exponentially at their lack of whining or complaining in relation to the pain the transition caused.

Drago went to meet up with Malachi so he could find out what he had seen. He would talk to Niara next. In different circumstances, I would've gotten the information firsthand from everyone, but I had priorities.

Sage and my baby's arrival were at the top of that list.

"Let's go," I told them, and I hurried to the employee parking lot. Reyn's car was where she said it would be. I used the code she'd given me to open the doors and snagged the shoes from the backseat. Christ. HEYDUDEs? They were a bit snug, but I wasn't bitching.

It was a mad dash to get to the room Reyn had texted that Sage was in. Along the way, the boys stopped in the waiting room to sit with Sloane and Niara.

A hot mess and knowing it, I barged in.

I wasn't prepared. I hadn't been there when Seth was born, and it had been almost eighteen years since Sam was born. Falina had also had an epidural, so I imagined it was a little different.

When Reyn left us to check on her other patients, Sage was ready for her to come back. She wanted my cousin to get the baby out of her in that moment. I had no idea what to say to that.

"I'm here, baby." I tried to sound sure as I took her hand in mine.

"Can you deliver a baby?" she asked, eyes wide and hinting at panic.

"Um, no."

She whimpered. Then all hell broke loose.

It didn't take long before a Sage I didn't know was making an appearance.

We hadn't talked about the vehicle that was following them because Sage was in active labor. Right now, she was safe, though not happy.

"I. Fucking. Hate. You," Sage snarled at me as she lifted her head from the pillow. Sweat soaked the hair around her face, leaving it stuck to her damp skin.

I was not a pussy.

But she was scaring me a little. If I didn't know better, I'd think she was possessed. No lie, I was waiting for her to stand up in the stirrups and talk in tongues. Maybe start spewing fire.

"I know," I murmured—because what else do you say when the woman you love is shoving your child out of her vagina?

A tired sob rang out when the contraction ebbed, and she clung desperately to my hand.

"I don't think I ever want to do this again," she panted, and my heart went out to her. No, I'd never make her do it again, and hell no, I'd never planned for this at my age—but fuck if that small part of my previously hardened heart wasn't doing weird things at the thought of holding my child soon.

Using a cool rag, I gently wiped her brow. Then I pressed an apologetic kiss to her head as I debated whether the most prudent course of action was to keep my mouth shut.

"It may not seem like it, but you're doing amazing, Sage," my cousin Reyn offered as she looked up over the massive arch of Sage's stomach from between her legs. "One more push and the head will be out."

"Oh God," Sage groaned as her grip on my hand increased. A quick glance at the monitor showed another contraction building. I'd made the mistake of narrating at first. She screamed at me to shut up. I think I was going to have a bruise from where she bit me when I told her it was a huge one—you know, like she couldn't tell.

It took several more contractions, a lot of pushing, and a little swearing before she brought a new life into the world. The second that cry filled the air, my chest clenched, and I knew I would tear down the world to protect that tiny helpless human.

"It's a girl!" Reyn happily announced.

I had a daughter.

Shit.

I was so fucked.

"She's beautiful," Sage murmured as she gently feathered her fingers over our daughter's dark fuzzy head, then put her tiny beanie back on. Little rosebud lips pursed, and I could see her mother in her, which confirmed how screwed I was. Her thick lashes fanned over full pink cheeks, and she was so peaceful that you would never know she'd recently been shoved through a birth canal.

"Here, Daddy." Sage lifted her slightly to hand her to me. "I think I want to call her Shae."

I looked at Sage, exhausted but gorgeous, and I smiled. "I like that." Then I returned my attention to my baby girl. She was so tiny compared to me that I was afraid I'd break her. Her soft skin was a pristine contrast to my fully inked arms.

Pulling her arms up, she arched her back and stretched inside the little baby burrito wrap. I held her securely, terrified she would wiggle her way out of my hold. She yawned, and her eyes peeked like she wasn't sure she wanted to open them. Then she closed them, blinked several times, and opened them wide. The dark blue of her irises held me captive as she seemed to be searching me clean down to my soul. I prayed she wouldn't see the darkness that lurked deep inside, because I would fight that darkness till my dying breath to keep her safe. Despite my reservations about being a dad to a little girl, my heart was full to bursting.

"Daddy loves you, beautiful," I whispered before pressing a kiss to her little head. Reluctant to let her go, I held her a bit longer. Finally, I placed her back in Sage's arms.

Once mom and baby were situated, I went to inform my family. My hands trembled as the magnitude of new fatherhood settled on my shoulders. I had a little girl.

"It's a girl," I dazedly announced to the waiting room full of my family and friends. My mom's hands covered her mouth as tears filled her eyes. Sam and Seth grinned before they jumped to their feet.

A body slammed into me, and I realized my cousin Evan held me in a massive bear hug. "I'm so happy for you, Adrien. Really. Maybe I'm selfish, but I'm glad you finally came home. I'm fucking thrilled that you have Sage, the boys, and now your little girl—but more so, I'm so damn relieved to have you back, man."

I swallowed the lump in my throat. "Me too" was all I could choke out, but I meant it. Something about being around him again was like having a part of myself back. The fact that I'd found Falina in his bed hurt, but the worst part was the betrayal I felt from him. It destroyed me that I lost everything in one fell swoop, but losing Evan had been like losing my brother all over again.

With each day that passed, my hardened heart softened. I finally wanted to be able to let go and move on.

"When you have time, we really need to talk," he murmured before giving me one last squeeze. He stepped back and blinked away the slight glisten from his tawny gaze. Finally, I nodded.

Everyone congratulated me, and a few at a time, they all stopped in to see Sage and Shae. It was late before everyone cleared out, leaving me and my little family, alone.

"Thank you for being here for me, boys," Sage told Sam and Seth with a tired smile and a heavy-lidded gaze. Shae was swaddled and resting on her mom's chest. Unable to stop myself, I trailed my finger over the curve of her pale pink cheek.

"Uncle Evan is giving us a ride back to the compound," Sam announced, and I paused.

After taking a deep breath, I slowly released it and nodded. It was strange, but it was fitting. After all, Evan had been as much a brother to me as my own had been. "Is he still in the waiting room?"

"Yeah, that's where he said he'd be," Sam replied.

"I'll be right back," I told them. I brushed a light kiss over Sage's plush lips and went down the hall. Evan was leaning against the wall, scrolling on his phone. He looked up and pushed off to stand square on his feet as I approached. His eyes narrowed slightly and his body practically trembled as he gave me a wary lift of his chin. I could tell the high emotions of Shae's birth had run away with him and now we were back to where we'd been before. I didn't like that.

"Evan."

"Adrien."

"You're right. We've wasted too many years thanks to a woman that wasn't worth it. Okay, and thanks to my stubborn-as-fuck nature too," I admitted as I tucked my hands in my pockets.

"I wanted to talk to you about that," he began, but I held up a hand.

"It's water under the bridge," I countered, but he shook his head as his eyes remained locked on mine.

"No, it's not. Because I didn't willingly sleep with her."

Despite saying I was letting it go, I huffed a humorless laugh.

"Adrien. I'm serious. She was staying with me at my house with the boys, yes. I didn't know everything that had happened. You were deployed, so it's not like I could just call you up. She led me to believe you guys had a falling out but that you'd work through it, and I had the room, so I let them stay with me."

"Generous of you," I muttered.

"Adrien," he pleaded and I sighed.

"Sorry."

He cleared his throat and ran a hand roughly over his mouth, then continued. "I have no idea how she knew you'd stop by. Or maybe she didn't, and it was dumb luck. Maybe she just planned to blackmail me and rub it in your face. Who knows? Except it worked out better for her than she could've imagined. She was able to drive that knife further into your heart."

Disbelief drew my brows down as I pressed my lips flat and processed what he said.

"You have to believe I'd never do that to you, man. After she put the boys to bed, we sat down and had a few drinks. Did we end up having too many? Maybe. But I remember climbing in my bed alone. Then I have bits and pieces of what happened but no clear picture. When I woke up, I was groggy, had a massive headache, I was nauseous, and my muscles ached." He stared at me.

"Are you trying to say you think she drugged you?" I asked with my eyes widening.

He shrugged. "Honestly, I have no proof, but yeah, I think so. One thing I know is that I didn't drink so much that I would've been that out of it and felt that hungover."

If what he was saying was true, Falina had been more conniving than I'd given her credit for. I couldn't believe she hated me that much. And for what?

I swallowed the lump that had lodged itself in my throat.

Because I believed him.

"Now I feel like an even bigger asshole than I did before," I muttered, chest tight and aching.

"Adrien, I didn't tell you that to make you feel bad. I needed you to know and believe that I never would've done that to you." The pleading in his gaze was mixed with a pain that I knew was reflected in mine.

All I could do was nod.

Then I took a step toward him, and he did the same. Finally, I was wrapping my arms around him. He was initially hesitant, but ended up embracing me back.

"Fuck, I missed you," he sighed. "For the past ten years, I've felt incomplete."

"Jesus, I know," I mumbled, full of emotion that I was having a hard time processing.

We separated, and I rubbed the back of my neck while he scratched his jaw.

"Thanks for giving the boys a ride back. You don't need to do that. Phoenix and Sloane would've taken them."

"I know, but it was out of their way. It's closer for me." He lifted a shoulder. "No worries."

"Come on, you can grab them and say goodbye to the girls." I motioned for him to follow me.

We walked side by side to the room, a comfortable silence between us.

After giving their love to Sage and Shae, the three of them left.

The nurse had brought me some linens and a pillow to sleep on the little couch that turned to a bed. I grimaced as I assessed it and came to terms with the fact that I was definitely gonna hang off the end. But there was no way I wasn't staying with Sage tonight.

It had been a crazy day, and I still didn't have much of an answer regarding the car that had followed them. Malachi had fallen back to try to get a license plate number, but the car had a license plate cover that obscured it. Illegal, but there nonetheless. Facet and Evan were trying to see what they could find out, and I had to be okay with that for the moment.

I sighed. The silence after such a hectic day seemed odd.

"Do you need anything?" I asked as I turned to Sage, but she was out like a light.

I gave each of my girls a kiss, then climbed into my makeshift bed. Lying flat on my back, my feet hung about a foot off the end. I sighed and rolled over. At least I could see Sage and ensure she and Shae were safe. I fell asleep staring at them.

Several times throughout the night, I woke up. A couple of times when the night shift nurse came in to do her rounds, then when Shae woke up hungry. Each time, I did what I could. The last time, I returned our little peanut to her bassinet after she'd been fed and climbed in next to Sage. I only intended to be there for a minute, but I woke up when there was a knock on the door, and Seth poked his head in.

I got up, and Sage grumbled in her sleep. Groggily, she frowned and blinked before sitting up with a yawn.

"Good morning, boys," she mumbled with a sleepy smile and a voice raspy from just waking up.

They came in with Sage's bag she'd had packed and ready for the last two months, a couple of boxes, and a gift bag. They handed one box and the bag to Sage. The last box, they gave to me. Evan stood behind them with a smirk he tried to hide.

"Huh? Why would you get me a gift?" I stared blankly

at the flat box. When the boys were born, I'd never gotten anything. It seemed weird. I wasn't the one who had popped out a kid.

"Because you needed it," Sam insisted. Something about the look on his face had alarm bells going off inside me.

Honored, yet still feeling like they were up to something, I cautiously lifted the lid and separated the tissue paper. Nestled inside was what looked like a black T-shirt. Once I unfolded it, I groaned. Evan and the boys cracked up laughing.

"Very funny," I deadpanned.

The shirt read "GIRL DAD" in bold white letters across the chest.

SIX

Sage

"LIVIN' ON A PRAYER"—BON JOVI

Because Shae was almost two weeks early, they had us stay an extra day for monitoring. Reyn suspected I may have gotten pregnant earlier than I initially thought, because Shae was perfect. She was exactly what a full-term infant should be.

"She's so precious," Reyn sighed as she looked her over, then she returned her attention to me. "I set your follow-up with the pediatrician I like to refer my patients to, but if for any reason you don't feel comfortable, you are free to switch."

I giggled. The pediatrician was her husband, and not a shifter, much to the family's initial disappointment. They soon fell in love with him—at least that's what Priscilla had told me. They'd been married since they were both in their residencies. "He came by earlier to check on her. I think he'll do fine."

She smirked. After we visited for a bit, she left.

Adrien went home to get the car seat because neither of us had thought to have the boys bring it when they came back this morning. I asked him to see if one of the guys could bring it, but he said they were all already tasked out or working. He took the floral-shop's worth of flowers and balloons home with him so we didn't need to have them in the SUV when we were bringing Shae home. I was getting her dressed in the girl outfit I'd packed. The boy one would either be gifted to someone, or get packed up "just in case."

Our room door was open because the nurse would be coming back shortly to remove my IV and go over my discharge instructions. I was dressed in real clothes again, so I didn't need to worry about someone seeing my bare ass if I got up.

"We're gonna go home as soon as Daddy gets back!" I told Shae as I wiggled her little feet. Her big, dark eyes seemed to study me intently.

A woman carrying flowers and a balloon walked past the door and paused. I glanced up.

"Oh! Hi, again!" She had on a pleasantly surprised smile as she stood in the doorway.

"Umm," I hesitated because, though she looked vaguely familiar, I couldn't place her. The way she was dressed ruled her out as anyone I would've met through the club. I knew Louboutins when I saw them.

"The craft fair. We both bought the star tree toppers. I'm Felicia. Sorry I didn't think to introduce myself yesterday, but it wasn't like I thought I'd see you again."

"Oh! I'm so sorry, I didn't recognize you at first. Pregnancy brain. Or that's what I'm calling it. I'm Sage." I chuckled. "Someone you know just had a baby too?"

"Well, it's nice to officially meet you, Sage. Yes, but I didn't get here in time, and she's been discharged. Hey, would you like these? It would save me from having to drive across town with them. I played hell keeping them out of my face on the way here. Corvettes weren't made for balloon deliveries." She winced.

I laughed. "I imagine not."

"So, you'll take them?" She gave me a comically hopeful gaze.

"You don't want to give them to your friend?"

"Pfft! I'll have them delivered this time. May I?" She motioned for permission to enter the room.

I waved her in, and she set the flowers on the bedside table that I'd pushed out of the way.

"Oh my goodness, she's precious!" she cooed.

Maternal pride made my chest swell. "Thank you."

"She looks just like you. What did you name her?"

"Shae Priscilla." I beamed.

"What a pretty name. Family name?"

"Her middle name is, yes."

"And your husband? I bet he's already entered into protective-dad mode." She chuckled.

Her assumption that I had a husband grated a bit, but I didn't know her, and even if I did, I didn't owe her an explanation. "Oh yes," I concurred.

I thought a flicker of surprise washed over her features, but she gave me a bright smile and I figured I'd imagined it. Either that or she was joking about the protective dad comment and didn't expect me to agree.

"Well, I better get going. It looks like you're almost out of here. Congratulations."

"Thank you." I gave her a genuine smile.

"Oh!" she called out as she stepped through the doorway. "Disregard the card."

I laughed and she joined me. Then she waved and I could hear her red-bottomed heels clicking as she walked away.

"What a small world, huh?" I asked Shae, though all she did was purse her lips and blink.

The nurse came back and finished discharging me. She told me to call when Adrien returned so she could wheel me out. While I waited, I fed Shae, and she immediately zonked out once her belly was full. Bored, I closed the door and laid down on the bed. I sent a text to Adrien.

Me: I'm ready to go as soon as you get back. Nurse already discharged me and the little miss. Love you

Adrien: I'm heading back now. Luv u 2, sexy

Not feeling the least bit sexy with a pad the size of a canoe between my legs and two more pads in my sports bra to keep me from leaking through it, I snorted a laugh. Then I sent an eye-rolling emoji. He returned the mad emoji. It cracked me up that my big, bad biker man was using emojis.

I hadn't meant to doze off, but I must've, because I jumped awake when I heard the door open.

"Hey, babe. I'm parked out front. I stopped at the nurse's station and your nurse is grabbing a wheelchair now." He kissed Shae's head, then sat on the bed next to me and ran the backs of his fingers over my cheek.

"Okay," I mumbled, still half asleep.

"Sage...."

"Yeah?"

"I really do think you're beautiful. Every minute of every day. I'm still amazed that you wanted an old guy like me after the shit I put you through, let alone love me like you do."

"Old? Pfft! You just turned thirty-six. That's not old."

He sighed. "Some days I feel eighty. I've lived a hard and ugly life. I'm so dark inside, and I don't know what I could've possibly done to deserve you and my children."

"Adrien, you're a good man, and you've had good reasons for the things you've done," I quietly assured him.

"All that matters is that you and the children believe that." He leaned closer and pressed his forehead to mine. But he turned his head and sat back up.

"Where did the flowers come from? I thought I brought all of them home." He got up and plucked the card from the little plastic fork thing that held it up.

"Oh, they weren't for me. A lady brought them to her friend, but she had been discharged before she got here, so she offered them to me. The card isn't for me either." I laughed but he didn't. "The weirdest part was that I had just seen her at the craft show yesterday. Small world, huh?"

He was frowning when he turned to face me, and he looked pallid.

"Are you okay?" I asked.

"She was at the craft thing too?"

"Yeah, we both bought an ornament from the same booth. We made small talk, and that was that. Then she came today to bring flowers to her friend, and I had the door open. She recognized me and gave me the flowers," I explained.

"This was no chance meeting," he practically growled, focused on the card in his hand.

"What?" I wrinkled my nose and tilted my head as I stared at him.

"Does that look like they were meant for someone else?" He handed me the card.

A—

Congrats on the new baby. Hope it's actually yours.

"Maybe her friend's name began with an A. Though, that's kind of a shitty thing to say to a friend. Adrien, what do you think is going on?" Trepidation crackled through me, and a chill skated down my spine.

His previously pale face flushed scarlet. "I don't know, but I'm damn sure going to find out."

The nurse came in pushing the chair, but he was busy on his phone so she patiently waited. Then he slipped it in his back pocket and slung my bag over his shoulder.

I finished buckling Shae into the car seat, and she slept through the entire ordeal. "Ready."

"Okay, Ms. Bennett, let's spring you!" The nurse's sunny smile was contagious.

Adrien lifted the seat with one hand, and my ovaries

exploded at seeing him carrying his infant daughter. The nurse sighed over my shoulder.

"I know, right?" I snickered.

"You lucky woman," she whispered to me.

We shared a laugh as she rolled me out of the room. As we passed the nurse's station, Adrien left the flowers sitting on their counter and kept walking.

Once we reached the front of the hospital, Adrien left Shae with me and ran to pull the SUV up. He buckled the car seat base in, then clicked the seat into it for the nurse to check that it was secure. Through it all, he doted on me and Shae. The nurse waved goodbye and went back inside.

He leaned in to kiss me, but instead of a light brush, he lingered. My heart raced as his tongue teased my lower lip. I opened and our tongues danced and glided together.

By the time he broke free, I was panting and clutching the front of his shirt.

"I love you," he murmured. "Thank you for having my baby."

I burst out laughing. He grinned in return.

"You're welcome?"

He teased the tip of his nose along mine, then stepped back and shut the door with a quick glance around. I watched him round the truck to the driver's side, and my heart nearly burst. How this ended up being my life, I hadn't a clue.

By the time we got back to the compound, Shae had woken up and was a little fussy. Adrien helped me climb down, then lifted Shae out. When I started toward the clubhouse, he grabbed my hand and shook his head.

Confused, I drew my brows together, but he tugged me gently behind him. That's when I realized he had parked at the end of the clubhouse in the spot closest to the tiny house village.

Excitement filled me. "It's done?"

"Yep."

We went up the steps to the small front porch, and he opened the door. I stepped inside, and tears filled my eyes.

"Welcome home!" everyone shouted. There were bunches of pink balloons everywhere. Some were from the hospital, but there were so many more.

"Thank you all so much," I cried. I sniffled. "I'm sorry, I'm still a little emotional."

"Okay, everyone out," Adrien commanded as Shae began to fuss. He set her on the gorgeous leather couch we'd picked out weeks before and lifted her into his arms.

When the guys tried to crowd around him, he twisted her away from them with a grumpy scowl. "No. You saw her in the hospital. She needs to eat, and Sage needs to rest."

I hid my smile behind my hand, but the guys weren't so courteous. They chortled at the overprotective behavior of their president, but they filed out after giving me a hug. They all told me they were happy to have me home. Blade was last, and his hug lasted a little longer than everyone else's.

Adrien cleared his throat, and Blade snickered. *He's so jealous*, he said into my thoughts.

"Stop it," I whispered back.

When he let me go, he clapped Adrien on the shoulder. "Congrats, Dad. I'm really happy for you both."

Sam and Seth had previously been tutored, but they recently started private school, so they weren't home yet. "I can't believe you got it done so quick," I said as I walked through the small home. I shivered, and Adrien cursed.

"Shit, here, you go in the bedroom and feed her. I'll go around and close the windows. I was trying to air out the paint smell before you guys came home." He followed me into our bedroom where I sucked in my breath.

"This is beautiful," I gushed as I ran my hand over the quilt made in shades of turquoise and black.

"My mom made it. I knew that pink was your favorite color, but I couldn't have a pink comforter on our bed. That was a bit much, but I know you also like turquoise and figured that was a good compromise." If I wasn't mistaken, he flushed as he glanced down at it.

"I love it. I'll thank your mom while I'm feeding Shae." I stood on my tiptoes and kissed his cheek.

He grabbed me by my hair, twisting it slightly to tilt my head up. When his lips crashed to mine, I whimpered. Completely lost in his kiss, I was absolutely oblivious to the world around me until Shae let out a very upset cry. We broke apart and I smirked.

"I see how things are going to be," I mockingly scolded my daughter as I took her into my arms.

"Fucking hell, it's gonna be a long damn six weeks," he muttered. One last brief kiss, and then he left me to feed the hungry little beastie.

I could hear him closing windows as I settled on my side and freed my breast. Shae greedily latched on and began voraciously sucking like she hadn't eaten in days. As she ate, she stared up at me, and I stroked her fuzzy dark hair. She was amazingly perfect, and I was totally in awe of her. The thought that Adrien and I created her and I'd carried her for nine months was mind-blowing.

"You're my little miracle, and I'll never treat you like my mom treated me. You'll always be Mommy's little princess."

She curled her itty-bitty fingers around one of mine and squeezed.

I smiled and my heart nearly burst.

SEVEN

Raptor

"THUNDERSTRUCK"—AC/DC

The second I had the windows shut, I checked on my girls. Sage was smiling serenely at Shae, and I was overcome with emotion. If I thought I'd lay down my life for Sage when she was pregnant, I'd now slaughter anyone who tried to harm her or any of my children.

Silently, I walked away and went out onto the front porch. I called Facet.

"Hey, brother. I'm guessing you're calling to see what I found out about the ex?" That was what he led with—he didn't even say hello.

"Yeah. And I appreciate you doing this for me. Hopefully, I'll have my own computer geek soon," I teased.

"You say I'm a geek like it's a bad thing, big boy," he returned in a mock-sultry tone that I couldn't help but laugh at.

"What have you got for me?"

"The ex has left the country. Flew out this morning—after she dropped off the flowers, I'm guessing. She joined her husband in Cuba. I can hack into their security system and set it up to notify you when she gets back. But more disturbing is what I found out about him."

"What the fuck? My search when she first married him came up with nothing but a rich fuck who had more money than brains. What the hell is he up to now?" I grumbled.

"It seems that Mr. Big-Bucks has rather perverse taste in his entertainment. His business trips are rarely actually for business. Turns out, he frequents countries that have child brothels," he grimly explained.

"What?" My question was deadly calm, but my teeth were clenched so hard, I was in danger of cracking one.

"Yeah, you heard me. He's one sick fuck. Seems the FBI has been watching him, but they haven't been able to pin him down with anything yet," he explained. I could hear his fingers flying over his keyboard.

"Think you could maybe anonymously help them out with that?"

"Oh, I think that could be arranged," he smugly replied.

"I'll pay Ankeny's going rate for it."

He snorted. "Brother, I already talked to Venom and filled him in. He said this one is on the house."

"I can't let you do that," I argued.

"Yeah, Venom said you'd say that. He told me to tell you tough shit, and said if you didn't like it, you could come back and try to kick his ass."

I couldn't help but laugh because I could hear my friend saying that. Though I was settling into my role as president here, I missed my brothers back in Ankeny. Maybe that made me a pussy, but I didn't give two shits. They were my family for years. They'd forgiven me for hiding the fact that I was a shifter. They understood that it wasn't because I was truly hiding it—it was because I wanted to completely turn my back on my past.

A decision that I now knew was a misguided mistake.

"Thank you. I appreciate that."

"Anytime," he assured me.

We ended the call, and I called Venom.

"Figured you'd be calling," he said with a chuckle when he picked up.

"You're an asshole, but thank you."

"You know damn well I'm not charging you for a damn thing."

"That's bad business," I countered.

"That's brotherhood. Now I hear you're home with the little one and Cookie."

"Sage," I corrected. I didn't agree with her going by

Cookie anymore because she was a different person now. She was mine.

"I'm happy for you, brother."

"Thanks, man. I appreciate that."

We chatted for a while about his family and how his grandma kept asking when I was coming back. The woman was a shameless flirt when it came to me, but I knew it was harmless.

I'd already checked in with Ares and Phoenix who were watching George Horacio's house. Now I had a pretty valid suspicion that Falina might've been the one following the girls the day Sage went into labor. But why? What was she hoping to accomplish?

A week later, we were on our way to my parents' house for Sunday dinner. Sam and Seth were in the backseat, flanking Shae's car seat and keeping her entertained. For two boys not raised with children other than themselves, it surprised me how good they were with her.

"She smiled at me!" Seth excitedly announced.

"She's not smiling at you, it means she has gas," Sam snickered.

"What? Ew!" Seth grimaced as he leaned closer to her. "I can't believe you just farted and laughed about it."

Sam chortled and Sage giggled. It was music to my ears, because she'd been so frazzled over the past few days.

Sage was doing great physically, but mentally and emotionally, she was wiped. Shae had been fussy as hell, and the only thing that seemed to put her to sleep was going for a ride. I hadn't been as much help as I wanted to be because we were trying to finish up the rest of the cabins.

We had done the touch-up and trim painting today. It would finish drying overnight, and we should be able to start moving everyone in tomorrow. The furniture I'd ordered for the remaining cabins would be delivered in the afternoon.

"I wish your mom would've let me bring something. I don't feel right showing up empty-handed." Sage chewed on her lip.

"We're bringing her grandchildren, that's all she's worried about. Besides, I guarantee she made enough to feed an army," I assured her as I gave her hand a gentle squeeze.

After we parked, everyone piled out of the vehicle, and I grabbed Shae in her little car seat. Sage hooked her hand in the crook of my arm, and we went inside. The scent of my mom's apple pie filled the house, and a satisfied grin lit my face.

"Give her to me!" Mom insisted the second we stepped into the kitchen. She had clearly already been doting on the boys, because they were sitting at the table with hot cocoa. When I set the car seat on the table to unbuckle Shae, Mom nudged me out of the way and took over.

"Oh, look at her! I think she's already grown since the day she was born. I can't believe you kept her from me for so long."

I huffed. "I didn't keep her from you. You are more than welcome to come to our place."

"To your biker commune?" She snorted.

"It's not a commune, Mom. And you know our house is done. Well, the temporary one anyway."

"Was the quilt okay?" she asked Sage as she snuggled Shae to her shoulder. "Adrien told me you would like the colors. If I didn't want to surprise you, I could've asked, but I wanted it to be a nice housewarming gift."

"It was stunning, and I was honored. Thank you," Sage told her, and Mom beamed.

Dinner went well, and dessert was my mom's apple pie, which made my fucking day.

"Do you mind taking Shae so I can help your mom clean up?" Sage asked, and my answer was to take my baby girl in my arms.

"I never mind taking her. Just don't overdo it—it's only been about a week since you gave birth," I instructed with an arched brow.

"Yes, sir," she whispered. The impish gleam in her eyes told me she knew exactly what those two words did to me. Us not being able to do anything about it, made me growl in frustration. My gaze narrowed, and she stood on her tiptoes to kiss me. I watched her ass sashay over to the sink.

I shook my head and glanced down at my little girl. "She's gonna get it for that," I whispered conspiratorially. Then we went out to the living room where my dad was watching Sunday night football. Gently, I set Shae in his arms. He grinned.

We weren't out there long when my phone chimed with one text message, then more. "What the fuck?" I muttered. Before I sat, I pulled my phone out. I didn't get the message thread open before I heard my dad suck in a sharp breath.

"Adrien...," he warned. I glanced at him in his recliner

with Shae snuggled up to him. He held his phone in his hand as he stared at the screen, then up at me. Something in the way he'd said my name had me opening the text from an unknown contact with trepidation.

"Please tell me you didn't get these too," I wheezed.

"Your mom's phone went off at the same time," he said in a strangled tone.

I practically flew out of the chair and into the kitchen.

EIGHT

Sage

"HATE MY LIFE"—THEORY OF A DEADMAN

The visit was going better than I hoped. Shae had been so fussy over the past week that I was worried it would make for a hectic time. Thankfully, she was fascinated with her grandparents and had been an absolute sweetheart the whole time. While her grandpa held her, I helped Priscilla clean up after dessert.

Multiple phones started pinging repeatedly. I didn't pay much attention until Adrien ran into the kitchen and reached for his mom's phone that she had already picked up. "Mom! Don't—"

"Oh. My." She blinked and looked a bit in shock. Then she lifted her gaze to Adrien and then me with her brows pinched. "Why does this look like Sage?"

My blood ran cold, and my gaze darted to Adrien, who looked green. Eyes a bit wild, he swallowed hard. Then he mouthed, "I'm so fucking sorry."

"What is it?" There was no hiding the tremor in my voice.

Adrien hung his head.

"She has a right to see this, but what I don't understand is why someone would send them to me," she told him.

"They sent them to me and Dad too," he mumbled.

"Oh sweet Jesus," she whispered.

When she held out her phone to me, my hand was shaking.

Never in a million years would I have expected to see at least seven images of me dancing on the stage back in Iowa. Mortified didn't come close to describing the feeling that washed through me as I flipped through each image.

"I...I...I," I stammered, but couldn't form a sentence to save my damaged soul. My first instinct was to grab Shae and run, but my feet were frozen to the floor. Tears streaked my face. Adrien plucked the phone from my hand and handed it back to his mom. He wrapped me tightly in his arms and held me close to his chest with his chin resting on the top of my head.

From the corner of my eye, I saw his mom quietly leave the kitchen. Then I heard softly murmured voices. God, please don't let the boys have gotten them too.

In shock, I couldn't do anything but cry. That was the last thing I wanted them to know about me, and actual visuals were worse. Holy shit. My baby's grandfather had seen me practically naked.

"Adrien, who would do that? Those were taken shortly after you and I started our... relationship." My spine stiffened, and I pushed back to look him in his eyes. "In fact, I remember that night, but I had no idea they were taken. Several rich assholes attended that night. Didn't tip for shit. Several had women with them who looked bored as hell and turned their noses up at us. In fact, I think a few left in a huff. Do you think it was one of them? No one touched their men. And how would they know to send those pictures to you and your parents? Tonight of all nights when we're all together? Adrien, how did that happen?"

Hysteria raised the pitch of my voice with each question. Panic was zinging through me, bouncing off my insides, shredding everything with the force of its momentum. My heart was pounding so hard, I was afraid it would break through my chest cavity.

"We're going home."

Numbly, I followed him as he held my cold hand in his massive one. On autopilot, I buckled Shae in, and she immediately started to cry. Priscilla watched me with sympathy, and I avoided eye contact the best I could. When I picked up the car seat, Adrien took it from me. "I've got it," he gently assured me.

The boys came down from where they had been playing video games upstairs. Unsure of what was going on, they glanced at each of us, then at each other.

"Thank you for dinner," I choked out. His mom approached and cupped my face.

"You are welcome here any day. I'm sorry such a wonderful evening ended this way. Please don't feel like we judge you for what you did for a living." She said it softly enough that I know she meant it for me, but to my ears, it sounded like she screamed it.

All I could do was nod, then I stepped out onto the porch. I trembled in the cold, but it had nothing to do with the frigid temperatures. The screen door opened, and Sam put my jacket around my shoulders.

Nervously, I wet my lips. "Did you and Seth get them too?"

His confused frown told me he had no idea what I was talking about. *Thank God.*

Adrien came outside, carrying Shae covered with her fluffy pink blanket. He was such a great dad.

We all loaded up in the SUV and left. Staring sightlessly at the dash as I worried my hands in my lap, I didn't see a thing we passed.

Adrien reached over the center console and separated my hands so he could hold my left one.

"Baby, I'm going to find out who sent those." The underlying warning was evident without him vocalizing it.

He was going to get revenge.

When we got back to the house, I fed Shae, and thankfully, she went right to sleep. I gently placed her in the bassinet we were using for the time being. I was hoping that we might have our actual house done before she outgrew it, but now I wasn't sure. Since she'd come a little early, we'd barely gotten this one done before she was born. Once she fell asleep, she slept through almost anything, but when she was awake, she was a handful.

The boys were out in the living room, watching a movie,

but I didn't feel like I was very good company. I quietly paced the small space. The bedroom door opened, and Adrien slipped in. He stopped in front of me and gently brushed my hair back.

"Hey, I'm going to take care of this. I know it was awkward, but neither of my parents care that you were a stripper. They know you as a person, and they love you. I think if you'd been a bank robber, they might've had a problem," he joked as he tried to cheer me up.

I was still shaking so bad, I literally felt on the verge of shattering. Like I was one step away from breaking down and never being able to come back from it. No matter how much I told myself I needed to get my shit together for Shae, I was slipping.

He leaned down and kissed me gently. Desperate, I grabbed his hair and pulled him in for a wild kiss. The feel of his tongue sliding along mine grounded me. He tangled his hands in my hair and took over. When he broke free, he kissed along my cheek and jaw before he teased along my neck with his teeth.

"Adrien," I whispered as I held him to me—needing him to get me under control.

He pushed my shirt up and pulled my sports bra up. The pads went flying. "You already fed her?"

I nodded and he growled before he lifted me to the bed.

"You focus on me. You hear? No noise. Shae is sleeping and the boys are out there."

Again, I nodded.

"Good girl. Hands up on the headboard rails." I obeyed

without question. When he took over, my mind was free. I trusted him to take care of me and keep me safe. He silently opened his bedside table drawer and pulled out a long scarf that he quickly and efficiently used to bind my hands to the rail. Then he pulled my panties and leggings off in one fluid motion.

"We can't—" I started but his sharp stare silenced me.

"You have to trust me to take care of you and know that I would never do anything to hurt you."

Swallowing hard, I whispered, "Okay."

His mouth and hands roamed over my skin, leaving goose bumps in their wake. He gently circled my nipples with his tongue and nipped at the swells of my breasts until I was writhing, aching to rub my clit against something—anything. It was a serious feat of willpower not to whimper.

When he slowly worked his way closer to where I desperately needed him, I panted as quietly as I could. The second he flicked my clit, then latched on, I had to hold my breath to keep from screaming. I gripped the scarf tightly and hung on for dear life.

He brought me to the edge several times before he finally gave me the release I needed. I exploded. A week without his mouth on me was too damn long. As the pulsing slowly subsided, I was left relaxed and almost drunk with satisfaction.

"Better?" he whispered in my ear.

"Mm-hmm," I hummed.

He released my hands and stashed the scarf, but I was too boneless to move. He softly chuckled as he dressed me again and carefully pulled my bra back over my boobs. When he put clean pads in it to cover my nipples, I wanted to cry at his thoughtfulness.

"Love you, baby," he whispered before he pressed his lips to my forehead.

"Luh you too," I mumbled as I rolled to my side and curled up. Vaguely, I was aware of him covering me and leaving the room before I fell into a peaceful sleep.

NINE

Raptor

"BREAKDOWN"—SEETHER

The moment I got Sage settled down—at the detriment to my own cock—I went into the clubhouse. I'd given instructions to Sam and Seth to check on Sage and Shae periodically before I left.

Filled with anger at what we were about to discuss, I shoved the chapel door open. My brothers sat at the table waiting.

"Thank you all for coming last minute," I stated as I took my seat. I filled them in on what had happened. We called Facet on speaker and told him about the situation. It took him all of five minutes to have an answer—sort of.

"The images were sent from the same burner phone that belonged to whoever hired the hit man—the same number he was supposed to send pictures of Sage's dead body to."

"Fuck!" I roared.

Facet spoke slowly and in a manner that told me he'd found something. "I don't think it was George Horacio."

"Why?" I demanded.

"Well, probably because he was fucking some chick when the messages were sent. Goddamn, I could make a killing off these videos. Who has a security camera in their bedroom?" I could hear the disgusted surprise in his voice. "Annnnd because the burner was being used internationally when they were sent."

My nostrils flared but other than that, I didn't move for several heartbeats.

"I'm going to kill her."

"Whoa, what? Who?" Blade snapped.

"Falina," I bit out between clenched teeth. "Can you pinpoint where it was used?"

The guy we caught said he was supposed to send pictures to the person who hired him and me. It was her? *Falina* hired him? I was reeling. I knew she was nuts, but I had no idea she was downright evil.

"I can't trace the phone at this moment because it appears to be shut off. But I can tell you that the signal originated in... Cuba."

Several of my brothers whispered or muttered, "Shit" and other expletives.

My chair crashed to the floor as I stood abruptly.

"Raptor?" Facet called out over the speaker.

"Brother, you can't go into Cuba." Gator gripped my arm firmly as he looked at me with disbelief in his gaze.

"Oh, I don't plan to. She'll come home sooner or later, and I'll be waiting. It will give me time to plan."

"Let us help you. Don't do this alone," Gator pleaded. "That's what we're here for. We have each other's backs, right? And that includes our families."

Breathing like I'd run a marathon, I ground my teeth. Finally, I nodded.

He sighed in relief. "Okay, so we make a plan."

"I'm going to work on a few things, but you guys call me if you need anything else," Facet chimed in.

"Roger that," I muttered.

"I think we should fly in some backup," Phoenix firmly suggested.

"Without knowing a timeframe, that could be tough," I replied as I gripped my hair and tugged in frustration.

"What about bringing Drago or Evan in?" Gator suggested.

"No." My answer was firm and definitive. I was not pulling my family in to bail me out again. Evan and I were mending fences, but I'd already asked so much of them. Though they likely wouldn't complain, I didn't want anything more that could be tied to my clan.

"What if they stayed here with our families?" Phoenix asked, seemingly reading my mind.

For a moment I wanted to refuse, but I knew I'd need

every many I could get when we went after Falina and her husband. Finally, I nodded. "I'll call Evan."

We sat there for several hours, and by the end of it, we had a plan. Maybe not a great one, but it was a plan.

The minute Facet notified us that Hatham's private jet had landed, we were on our way to their estate. Parked in the van, we waited in the driveway of the house down the street. We double-checked, and they were on vacation in the Bahamas, so we were safe. The dark-tinted windows concealed us from nosey neighbors, and Facet had already intercepted the cameras that monitored the driveway.

It wasn't long before a town car pulled up to their house. Except it was only Falina that got out. The driver went around to the trunk and removed her suitcase. He followed her to the door and deposited the suitcase inside before giving her a wave and departing. Lights flicked on as she went through the house.

"I'm going in. Facet gave me the okay that the staff has gone home for the night, and the cameras are on a loop, so we're clear," I announced as I climbed out of the van.

"Maybe we should find out where Hatham is first," Blade interjected.

"I don't care. If he shows up, it becomes a murder-suicide because he's a disgusting piece of shit that fucks children," I replied.

Blade had nothing to say to my cold reply.

"We'll take our places," Gator told me as he shot a

warning glance at Blade. We checked that our comms were working and dressed in head-to-toe black, then we spread out around the house. I went to the back doors that I'd used during my last visit.

"Bro, you need to be rational," Gator said when we were alone and skirting around the massive house.

I stopped and turned to face him.

"I'm being perfectly rational," I calmly argued.

"Jesus," he muttered, but we resumed our mission.

Once we scaled the brick-and-stucco privacy fence, Gator unlocked the gate for the rest, then waited in the deepest shadows. I saw Phoenix, Blade, and Torque split up and take their places. Tigger gave me the signal that he was in position out front. One Short had stayed back with Evan and Drago to keep watch over the women. Niara, Sloane, and her mom had come over to keep Sage busy and safe in case things went south.

After picking the lock, I let myself in with hardly a *snick* of the door latch. The lack of alarms told me Facet had indeed set things up perfectly for us. I owed the Ankeny boys more than I could repay.

I followed the clink of crystal into Hatham's study. The door was cracked open, and I pushed it enough to see that Falina was alone and had her back to the door. She raised a glass and took a drink.

"You might as well come in," she said, and I stepped into the room.

"Expecting me, were you?"

"I figured I had a visit coming" was her noncommittal reply as she turned to face me.

"Why would you do that? What were you hoping to accomplish?" I demanded.

"What exactly are you referring to?"

I started with "You hired a hit man to kill Sage" as I glared at her.

A heavy sigh left her before she took another drink. "I was hoping to get rid of her before you got attached."

"What the fuck?"

She boldly met my gaze.

"I saw you in Iowa with that woman, and I immediately knew she was different." Falina paced, then stopped to stare out the window of the study.

"You were stalking me?" I asked incredulously.

She paused and gave me a sardonic stare. "No. I actually had no idea you were there. At first, anyway. Until several years ago, when we traveled to Iowa for Hatham to meet with one of his business associates. They were looking at opening a gourmet restaurant chain in Des Moines—the last place I thought you'd be. It may surprise you to know that I didn't keep tabs on you at first. I thought I'd be prepared if I ever saw you again, but I wasn't. It was then that I hired someone—just to check on you. It was for my own peace of mind."

"Okay, well, that's stalking me," I explained as if to a five-year-old.

She pinched the bridge of her nose. Then she dropped her hand to her chest.

"It wasn't constant. Adrien.... God, I never stopped loving you. All the years we were apart, I was okay with the other women because they didn't mean anything. Until the last trip when I saw you with her." She resumed her pacing. Her hands fluttered nervously to her hair, then her necklace and earrings.

Wary, I watched every move she made. I remained silent and let her continue.

"I immediately knew she was different. I saw it in the way you looked at her when she was onstage that night. Yet, I could see she was so wrong for you. You were making a terrible mistake, but it seemed she had bewitched you." The corners of her mouth turned down and her brows pinched in the center as her gaze pleaded with me to understand.

Except—I couldn't. No amount of explanation could make me understand her insanity.

"Falina… did you really think I'd have anything to do with you again?" I stilled and my breath froze in my chest. But she didn't answer my question. Instead, she tangentially rambled.

"I found out what he was doing," she replied with a tremble of her lip. "I couldn't be with him anymore."

"Who? And what the fuck does that have to do with me or Sage?" I asked, giving her a flabbergasted glare. She wasn't making any sense. It was as if she had completely unraveled.

She cocked her head as if she didn't understand why I wasn't following what she was explaining. If there was any question that she was living in her own little crazy world, it was now perfectly apparent.

"The business trips Hatham took. They weren't for business. Well, not like you'd expect. He brought me along and happily handed me his credit card to go shopping while he went and purchased sex with children—in foreign whorehouses that cater to that kind of perversion. I was sick to my stomach. Then I found out you were back. It was a sign, and I knew what I had to do." A slightly hopeful light flickered in her dark eyes, but then extinguished and her shoulders drooped.

"What was that?" I asked calmly, playing along to get her to open up—because I wanted answers.

"I had to ensure she couldn't come between us," she explained, but I was still confused. I waited.

She dropped her head to stare at her folded hands. Then her eyes closed, and she huffed a breath from her flared nostrils. When she opened them and lifted her tearful gaze to lock it on me, she looked tortured. "God, I feel like I'm two different people at times. I have no excuse for what I did. Looking back on it, I have no idea what I was thinking... where my head was. I hired a hit man. For Sage and Hatham. Except he disappeared before the job was done. Though I believe Hatham deserved that a million times over, your... Sage... didn't. I did a lot of thinking after I sent those pictures. If I could've taken them back, I would've. You were right... I was a despicable human for what I did to you and the boys."

Shit! Tigger is down! Incoming! Blade's voice echoed in my head.

I had no time to react before the door flew open, and Falina's husband, Hatham, barged into the room. Brandishing a pistol, he was disheveled, his eyes bloodshot and crazed. Wherever he'd been obviously wasn't up to his usual standards.

"You bitch!" he spat at Falina. "There was a man outside! Did you talk to the FBI? Do you realize they're watching us, and they've seized the majority of our assets? They picked me up as I was leaving my office. I've spent the last two hours being interrogated! And I come home to find you all cozy in *our* study with your *ex-husband!*"

Thank you, Facet.

Without taking his eyes from us, he moved behind the desk. The gun wavered between me and Falina. He flipped the painting from the wall, revealing a recessed safe. Frantic, he slapped his hand over the biometric pad. It opened, and he grabbed Falina's designer tote from the desk and dumped the contents onto the floor. Blindly, he pulled stacks of cash and what looked like several passports from the safe, then filled the bag and every pocket he had.

Once the compartment was empty, he sneered. "I always knew you didn't love me—it was always *him.* Did you have any idea how you ripped my heart out? There wasn't anything I wouldn't have done for you. But you fucked up when you went to him and then worse when you turned me in. You both fucked up by screwing me over."

"I didn't talk to anyone! And I'm not having an affair!" Falina snapped.

And how could he profess to love her so much when he was traveling to child brothels in other countries? Maybe the same way she could say he was sick but look the other way while happily blowing his money.

"Hatham, I don't know what you think is going on, but I would never touch her," I cautiously began, trying to reason with him as I took a tentative step toward him. Jesus, they were both nuts.

"You shut the fuck up! It was *always* you. A thorn in my side. I should've had you killed years ago." He leveled the gun at my chest, and I paused, raising my hands in surrender.

For fuck's sake!

The last thing I wanted to do was die. Focusing, I sent my inner hawk out to see where my brothers were. My remote sight showed me that Tigger had a head wound, but Gator and Torque were with him. I couldn't tell if he was alive. Ares and Blade were running toward the house. Returning to myself, my vision cleared, and I knew I only needed to buy a minute or two.

"I'm not going to try to stop you," I said, attempting to placate him.

His maniacal laughter filled the room as he backed toward the door. "Oh, I know you aren't. Because she's gonna watch you die, then we're leaving the country. I was able to buy us a window to fly out on the jet."

Like it was in slow motion, I watched his finger tighten on the trigger.

Falina cried out and threw herself in front of me the second he fired the gun. She fell back into my chest, knocking me off-balance.

There was a snarling roar, and a powerful golden cat charged in the door and pounced on him. Sharp claws and wicked teeth sank in and ripped at his flesh. Blood sprayed across the cream-colored rug in a macabre display as he screamed and tried to fight the angry cat off.

I pushed Falina's limp body off me and checked for a pulse.

Well, fuck. He goddamn killed her before I could. Guess we were going to have a murder-suicide after all.

"Ares!" I shouted. The cat stopped, and its unusual blue eyes stared at me. Blood covered its face and paws. Hatham was an unrecognizable mess of shredded meat. *Fuck me.*

The cat snarled and hissed. Jesus fucking Christ. Just what I needed, a young shifter who didn't have full control of his animal. Fuck, mammals were tough to get a handle on. That told me he hadn't had a lot of experience with his transitions. "Ares, it's me, Raptor. Can you shift back?"

He spun and darted out of the room.

"Shit. Blade!"

"I'm here, but what the fuck was that?" Blade asked as he stared dumbfounded in the direction Ares had run.

"That was Ares, and Ox up in Minnesota has some questions to answer. Like why he didn't give me a heads-up," I grumbled as I ran a hand through my hair.

"Maybe he didn't know. It could come from his dad's side," Phoenix offered as he came in. The look in his eyes made me sit up and take notice.

"What's going on?" I braced myself for whatever shit-storm he was about to unleash.

"Tigger's in bad shape. I wish we had Angel here," Phoenix replied.

"What happened?" I asked.

"When Hatham pulled up, he caught Tigger and tased him. That in itself isn't bad, but it looks like he fell and whacked his face on the side of the house. He's bleeding pretty bad. Gator is doing what he can," Phoenix informed me. All I could do was nod.

"Ho-ly shit," Gator drawled when he stepped through the doorway.

"There's no way we can explain that." I motioned to Hatham's mangled form.

Blade walked over to him and scooped up Hatham's gun. He grabbed him by his blood-soaked hair, propped him in the chair, then took his hand, put the gun in it, and put it to his temple. We jumped a bit when Blade pulled the trigger. Then he walked through the house to the kitchen, grabbed a knife, and wrapped Falina's hand around it.

"There. Now Phoenix can torch the house, and it should look like a murder-suicide. Wait. Let me go out to the garage and check for a gasoline can." He left again.

"Is he okay upstairs?" Gator asked as he tapped his temple with a skeptical brow lift.

"That's relative." I shook my head. "How is Tigger?"

"Not good. Torque is gonna see if one of his buddies who used to be a medic in the army can come by the clubhouse—so we gotta get moving. He's not gonna say what happened. Not ideal, but…. Do you need to grab anything from Sam and Seth's rooms?" Gator explained, then asked.

"Cancel Torque's friend. I'll reach out to my dad and ask him to swing by." I pulled out my phone and made the call. After a quick explanation, my dad told me he'd be there.

"Pull the van around to the service gate so we can get Tigger loaded up, and then we'll finish this. Dad's on his way now. And no, we got everything when they moved in with me."

"Then let's roll."

Blade came back and splashed gasoline around before Phoenix worked his magic. Then we grabbed the stuff Ares left behind and hauled ass back to the clubhouse. We passed several fire-and-rescue vehicles on the way to the house. You could see the flames for miles.

"Anyone heard from Ares?" I asked once we were on the highway. He never came back to the house, and I was a little worried that someone would see him and shoot him. It wasn't every day that people saw a mountain lion running through the rich neighborhoods of Dallas.

Everyone shook their heads. "Fuck," I muttered.

"Did you know Ares was a shifter? I figured you guys could sense each other or something," Phoenix called up from where he sat with Tigger in the back of the SUV. Blade was driving, and he cast me a sidelong glance.

"Hell no, I didn't. I wouldn't have had an issue with it.

It would've been nice to have the heads-up, though. Now I understand how everyone felt up in Ankeny when they found out about me. Because I had my reasons, I can only imagine that he does too. What I do know is that guy hasn't shifted much. The scary thing is, if he can't control it, someone's gonna get hurt," I explained.

"You don't owe us an explanation. I just wondered if you knew," Phoenix clarified.

"Where do you think he could've gone?" Gator asked.

"That's just it. I have no idea," I grimly admitted. "How's Tigger?"

"Weak thready pulse," Phoenix replied.

The screen of my phone lit up, and I glanced down. "Dad is at the compound."

"You can let him know we're about ten miles out," Blade told me as he turned on his blinker and glanced over his shoulder to switch lanes. He was driving like a bat out of hell, but if there was anything Blade knew other than torture and blades, it was vehicles. He never drove recklessly— each move was calculated and precise. Actually, the man knew a lot, but most people wouldn't suspect it. They saw his ink and his piercings and wrote him off as a tatted-up thug.

Now, he might be a little bit crazy, but his loyalty was a step above. I was glad Sage had him during the time I was a dumbass and left her behind.

My thumbs flew over the screen as I shot off the message to my dad.

It wasn't long before we were pulling through the gate

and up to the clubhouse. Torque, Dad, and One Short came out, carrying a litter. We carefully got Tigger onto it and rushed him inside.

"Okay, everyone out," my dad snapped. "I need space."

They took him into the small room we used as an infirmary. It was barely bigger than a janitor's closet, but the stretcher fit with a couple of feet all the way around. Once we finished all the cabins, we would convert one of the bunk rooms into the infirmary, and this would become storage. I missed the space we had in Ankeny.

We all shuffled out to the common area.

"How's Tigger?" One Short asked.

Surprise had me stopping in my tracks. There was a massive Christmas tree in the corner by the couch that came close to touching the ceiling. It was decorated and lit. Then tiny Christmas lights twinkled around the ceiling and along the bar. They were even woven behind the bottles at the bar.

"Holy shit. Who did all this?" Gator asked. None of us had noticed when we came in because we were too focused on Tigger.

"Prez's ol' lady was a slave driver," Torque replied with a smirk. "She had me, One Short, Sam, and Seth climbing ladders while she, Niara, and Sloane decorated the tree."

"Where the fuck are they now?" I asked, my hands propped on my hips.

"Your place. The boys are with them," One Short chimed in.

"I'll be right back." Tigger was in good hands with my dad, and I had a sexy, stubborn woman to speak to. If she had been on a ladder or carried heavy shit, I was going to spank the hell out of her.

Once I was outside, I stopped short. All of the cabins were trimmed with lights. Every single one. Even the ones we weren't done with.

I stormed with purpose to our home. Then I stomped up the steps and flung open the door. My frustration fizzled quickly when I walked in to find all of them laughing with Christmas music playing in the background. Five sets of eyes found me, and Sage's smile fell. Seeing that physically hurt.

"Adrien?" she asked. "What's wrong?"

"I…." Nothing else came out—I was at a loss for words. Instead, I cleared my throat. "A word?"

"O-okay," she stuttered, but she followed me into our bedroom while Sloane held Shae and everyone looked at me with mild trepidation.

Calmly, I closed the door. "Please tell me you didn't get on a ladder or lift anything heavy."

"Adrien. Give me a little credit. Please don't be mad. I needed this. It did wonders for getting my mind off everything." Her fists were propped on her curvy hips, and I couldn't help it—I grinned at the return of her sass.

"I fucking love you." It was all I could come up with.

But she smiled. And fuck, that smile was… everything. It lit her face and left her looking stunning. Breathtaking.

She threw herself into my arms and practically squeezed my head off. In all fairness, I might've made her back crack with as tightly as I held her against me.

"Now, tell me what happened."

I sighed. Then I explained what had transpired at Falina and Hatham's house—well, most of it. She'd been around the club long enough that she knew more than any other ol' lady and never breathed a word.

"She wanted to kill me?" Horror filled her pretty blue eyes as her lower lip trembled. "I'd never done anything to her. I didn't even know her."

"I'm convinced that she had gone off the deep end. With every layer I uncovered, it was more and more apparent." Then I told her what we'd discovered about Hatham and she visibly trembled.

She glanced over her shoulder toward the living area. The devastation in her stare when she returned her attention to me was almost palpable. "You don't think... you don't think he... h-hurt the boys, do you?"

Then what I knew of her past came back to me and revulsion roiled in my guts that this situation might be making her relive any of her childhood. I gathered her in my arms and held her close. Slowly, I smoothed my hand over the crown of her head and speared my fingers into her silken hair. "No, baby, I don't, but I'll sit down with them and discuss it. So there's no speculation."

A shudder shook her frame, and I wanted to engulf her in the protection of my body—shelter her from the world's evil.

"Jesus Christ. I don't even know what to say," she murmured.

"They're both gone now. That's all that matters to me," I replied.

"But she sacrificed herself to save you. So no matter how bad all the other shit was, I have her to thank that you're here in front of me. That's so fucked up. And I still can't believe she wanted to have me killed. All because we were together? Holy shit, I'm glad she wasn't successful." She pulled back to gaze up at me, eyes wide.

"Fuck, I know. Because the thought of losing you guts me. I need you, baby. And I don't only mean in my bed."

She smirked and shook her head.

"Well, guess what?"

"What?" I asked before kissing the tip of her nose and sending thanks out to the powers that be.

"I love you too."

EPILOGUE

Raptor

Though Sloane didn't celebrate Christmas, she joined us for the celebration and festivities. For her, it was Yule. I didn't care what anyone called it—it was a day we spent together. Except for Niara, who was with her siblings that had come to visit, it was the first family holiday we celebrated as a chapter. One Short even brought a chick he'd been seeing off and on.

When we were all sitting around the tree, drinking cocoa and eggnog—spiked for everyone except Sage and the boys—I took a moment to scan the room. My heart was happy. Settled. My parents were there, as was Evan. Phoenix held their little girl who was a few months old now and batting at his beard with uncoordinated swings while he teased her. She giggled, and the corner of my mouth kicked up. My mom had Shae snuggled into her neck, sleeping through most of her first Christmas.

I was 100 percent correct when I told Sage my family wouldn't give two shits about the fact that she used to be a stripper. They adored her because she made me happy and was a genuinely good person.

Sage came over and sat in my lap, draping her arms over my shoulders.

"Merry Christmas, you sexy thang," she drawled as she waggled her brows.

I chuckled. "Merry Christmas."

"This is nice," she murmured.

"Yeah. It really is. But I have one more gift for you."

"Oh, do you?" Her soft smile turned wicked, and she wiggled her ass against my cock. Of course, it wasn't enough that anyone else noticed, but my dick sure as hell did.

"Yeah, I do, but now I can't stand up unless I want everyone in the room to see my boner. Thanks for that," I grumbled, trying my best to keep my mouth flat.

"Any time," she purred, and I couldn't help it—I laughed.

"You need to go get it for me," I told her with a crooked grin.

"Where is it?" She glanced around.

"See that little green stocking hanging in the middle of the tree?" I pointed and she squinted as she followed the direction of my finger.

"Yes. When did you put that there?" Her suspicious gaze locked on my face. When I didn't answer, she lifted a brow.

"Just go get it," I urged. Nudging her up with my leg, I swatted her ass as she stood. Then I followed said ass with my lustful gaze as she wound through our family and friends to get there. Stocking in hand, she meandered back. The whole time, I could tell she was trying to feel it to figure out what it was. It was my turn to smirk because she never would.

When she returned to me, she dropped back into my lap, causing me to quietly groan. "You damn tease," I whispered.

"Can I open it now?" She batted her eyes dramatically.

All I could do was shake my head at her antics. "Yeah, baby, you can open it."

She fished inside the stocking and pulled out the flat little box wrapped in silver paper. Her cheeks heated, and she stared at me wide-eyed. "Please tell me this is PG."

A snort of laughter escaped me at her plea. "Yes. It is. But you can bet your sweet ass we're using the other gifts tonight."

She sucked in a sharp breath, and her lips parted as her pupils took over her light blue eyes. Looked like I wasn't the only one who was on the verge of implosion from no sex. Yeah, we had done some groping and oral, but it wasn't the same.

It had only been five weeks since Shae was born, but I knew Reyn squeezed her in a couple of days ago because she was taking a trip to the Cayman Islands with her family for the holidays. She'd given Sage the green light. I only knew because she told Sloane, who told Phoenix, who told me. Sometimes the club was a little like high school—at least with harmless things.

"Promise?"

"Fuck yeah, I promise. I would never do something like that to you. What we do behind closed doors is our business. No one else's."

"Oh thank God."

"Now open it."

Like a child, she ripped the paper off. She was oblivious to the pause in conversation. Nor did she notice that Sam had his phone focused on us.

The little white cardboard box was unassuming, and she shook it slightly. I chuckled. I'd intentionally switched the packaging. Couldn't be too obvious.

Finally, she lifted the lid. My chest squeezed in anticipation.

Her breath hitched as she lifted the cotton square. Then she looked up at me, mouth hanging open, and blinked away the glisten of tears that were welling. "Adrien," she whispered.

Carefully, I plucked the ring from the box. My fingers were so big, I was afraid I'd knock it to the ground or drop it. It took two swallows for me to get the golf ball-sized lump in my throat to move so I could speak.

"Sage Bennett, would you do me the honor of becoming my wife?" My heart was pounding so hard, it was almost exploding from my chest. I had never been so damn nervous in my life. It was a weird state of mind for me.

"You mean marry you?" she rasped, then cleared her throat.

"That is what we would need to do for you to become my wife," I deadpanned.

She splayed her hands over her chest. "I think I'm gonna hyperventilate."

Gently, I took her left hand in mine. "Baby? You're killing me, here. Can I get a yes or no from you?"

"Yes," she finally replied in a nearly soundless whisper.

Before she could take it back, I slipped the ring onto her finger.

With ragged breaths, she stared at her hand, and the ring caught the tree lights in its facets. Then she abruptly lifted her gaze to me. "Oh my God. I'm really gonna be your wife? Sage Krow?"

"Unless you've changed your mind in the last twenty seconds, yeah."

"Holy shit." She blinked a few times, looked at the ring, then at me. "HOLY SHIT!"

Before I could respond, she threw herself at me, peppering kisses all over my face. Everyone around us started cheering and hooting, drawing her attention. She still held my face in her hands as she looked at them over her shoulder and beamed. "I'm gonna be his *wife*!" she shouted.

Laughter filled the room, and they all said, "We know."

Later that night, when everyone was in bed, we locked all the doors and windows, then drew the curtains. We carried Shae's bassinet and set it in the living room, next to her oldest brother. Sam already told me he would listen for her and sleep on the couch. I loved my son for not asking why we needed a little of the night to ourselves.

In our room, I closed the door and rounded on my fiancée. "Strip."

Her usually bold and sassy demeanor calmed, and she did as she was told—all with a softly wicked tip of her lips. Slowly, I circled her. My fingertips blazed a path across her skin. She inhaled a shuddering breath, but remained still. Tenderly, I swept her hair to the side, exposing the slender column of her neck. I brushed my knuckle over the soft skin before bringing my mouth to hers. What started as a kiss turned to a taste before I bit hard enough to make her shiver, but not hard enough to hurt her.

"So delicious. What else do you have that would be delicious, Sage?"

She whimpered, and I chuckled darkly. "Answer me, or I'll do nothing but tease you all night."

"My pussy," she boldly replied.

"Mmm," I hummed. After sliding my hands from her shoulders to the crook of her elbows, I slowly pulled them together. The movement caused her perfect tits to push out. I'd prepared in advance, so I reached down to the bedside table for the red satin ribbon. Focusing, I took my time wrapping it from her elbows to her hands. Her shoulders strained as they arched back. "Too much?"

"No, it's okay for now."

"Good." Then I reverently worshipped her body. Crouching and kneeling, I licked and sucked on every exposed inch I could reach until she was quivering and whimpering. Then I unwound the ribbon to bring her arms in front of her where I wrapped her forearms and tied it at a bow at her wrists. Thanking the good Lord above for my height, I reached up and flipped a smoke detector cover down, exposing a heavy-duty loop. She'd never thought to ask why there were two smoke detectors, and I'd patiently waited for the day I could show her.

"Lift your arms," I commanded, and she obeyed. I snapped one end of the chain onto the loop, then the other so that I connected the ribbons at her wrists. Then I spent the next thirty minutes driving her crazy.

After her second orgasm, her head hung as she panted. I released her arms and scooped her up to lay her on the bed. Once I knew she was comfortable, I removed the red satin and massaged her muscles and joints with a softly scented oil. By the time I finished at her feet, she was moaning, tits pushed high as she arched off the mattress.

"Jesus, you're fucking amazing," I murmured as I dipped two fingers between her legs, coating them in her slick release. "Roll over. Ass in the air."

When she whined a bit as she slowly did as I said, I smacked the perfectly rounded globe of her ass. She hissed in a breath between gritted teeth. "No lagging, and no fussing. You do as I say when I say it—and you don't hesitate. Understood?"

"Yes, sir" burst from her lips.

I quickly undressed and climbed up to kneel between her spread knees. "God, I wanna fuck your ass," I muttered. "Can I fuck your ass, Sage?"

"Yes, you can do whatever you want to me," she obediently blurted out.

"That's right. I can do whatever I want, whenever I want, and wherever I want. Remember that promise?" I stole some of her pussy juices with my thumb, then pushed it past the tight ring of her ass.

"Yes."

Slowly fucking her ass with my thumb, I notched the tip of my cock at her opening and circled it in the slippery cum that soaked her pussy lips and the tops of her thighs. "Tonight, I think I'll just fill this tight cunt with my cum. What do you think, baby?"

"God, yes."

Because it had been a while, and I wasn't a pencil dick, I slowly worked my way in. With each shallow stroke, I fed my thick cock further into her tight sheath. Her face buried in the pillow, she clutched the quilt. I watched the tension and release of her muscles and the hold she had on the blanket to gauge how she was tolerating my invasion. When she pushed her ass toward me, taking everything I had to give her, I knew she was okay.

Hips rolling, I cautiously picked up the pace. With each stroke, I watched my length slide in and out. I made sure the wet coating she left on me wasn't mixed with blood. The last thing I would ever do is actually hurt her. My skill was in recognizing the difference between good pain and bad pain, then keeping her just on the good side.

"Adrien, oh fuck, Adrien, oh Christ," she chanted into the pillow as I drove harder. The flutter of her pussy walls told me she was getting close. When she clamped down on me, I braced myself. I didn't want to come quite yet.

Except when she clenched so hard that I thought she'd

break my dick off, I picked up the pace and fucked her with unleashed madness. Tighter and tighter, she squeezed.

My eyes crossed.

When she finally broke, and the pulsing of her hot, wet sheath became too much, I thrust deep and held. My balls tightened up and I shot my load in her. It seemed like I would come forever, but I couldn't stop. It wasn't until I was about to collapse that a shiver shook my frame, and I rested my face on her back. Her tight pussy kept squeezing me, and I groaned.

"Jesus Christ, woman. You're going to squeeze my dick off."

She laughed through her gasping breaths, and the movement pushed me out of her. "Fuck!"

With satisfaction, I watched my thick cum run out of her and slowly down her thighs. Like a goddamn caveman, I used my still hard length and gathered the cum, pushing it back inside her.

"We should've used something. My birth control isn't 100-percent effective until three months," she mumbled with her cheek smashed into the pillow.

"Does it make me an asshole if I said I don't care if I got you pregnant again?"

"Yes! Christ, give a girl a break. At least let my damn pussy recover and go back to normal."

I laughed. "Sweetheart, I hate to tell you, but I think you're tighter now than you ever were."

She snorted and the cum rolled out again. I growled and rubbed it into her skin, and then I pushed it back in again.

She was mine, and damn if I didn't want to mark her body as mine in the most primitive of ways.

"Are we always going to have amazing sex like this? Do you think it will get old?"

I rolled her over and wrapped my body around hers. "Not as long as I have breath in my body. What we have is a once-in-a-lifetime thing. I'm never going to grow tired of you, and I'm never letting you go. I'll probably die at ninety-seven with my cock buried balls deep."

Her laughter rang out, and I smiled.

"I love you, Sage."

She traced the ink on my chest with her fingertip. When she spoke, she paused and splayed her hand over my heart. "I love you too. Forever and for always."

I gathered her close and held her. We fell asleep like that. Then a knock on the door and a wailing little girl had me jumping out of bed and pulling my jeans on commando. I didn't even bother fastening them.

Sam stood outside the door, looking apologetic with his hair sticking up every which way. "I'm sorry, Dad. She's not having the bottle."

"It's okay, son. I'll take her to her mama."

Relief softened his face and his shoulders relaxed. Guilt hit me for a moment that I was partly responsible for his mother's death. Sam, Seth, and I had sat down the next day, and I broke the news to them. Initially, they had both been quiet. Seth had looked to Sam for guidance, then Sam had assured me it wasn't my fault. "I'm more sad that she was never who we needed her to be," Sam had softly explained.

My heart had broken for them, and I promised myself to always be the dad they needed.

"Goodnight," he said as he walked off. When he hit the base of the stairs, he glanced over the railing at me and grinned. "Hope I helped."

"Oh, yes."

His soft laughter filled the room as he climbed the stairs. I shook my head and brought Shae to her mother. I'd barely set her down next to Sage before our greedy little girl was madly rooting for her mama's breast. Without opening her eyes, Sage gathered her closer and situated her. Then she cracked one eye open.

"Thank you."

"Absolutely. Anything for my girls."

Bone-weary by then, I crawled up behind her and wrapped my arm around both of them. Though a year ago I would've never seen my life looking like this, I wouldn't give it up for anything.

With Sage and my children, I was home.

Royal Bastards MC Facebook Group
www.facebook.com/groups/royalbastardsmc

Website
www.royalbastardsmc.com

ROYAL BASTARDS CODE

PROTECT: The club and your brothers come before anything else and must be protected at all costs. CLUB is FAMILY.

RESPECT: Earn it & Give it. Respect club law. Respect the patch. Respect your brothers. Disrespect a member and there will be hell to pay.

HONOR: Being patched in is an honor, not a right. Your colors are sacred, not to be left alone, and NEVER let them touch the ground.

OL' LADIES: Never disrespect a member's or brother's ol' lady. PERIOD.

CHURCH is MANDATORY.

LOYALTY: Takes precedence over all, including well-being.

HONESTY: Never LIE, CHEAT, or STEAL from another member or the club.

TERRITORY: You are to respect your brothers' property and follow their Chapter's club rules.

TRUST: Years to earn it… seconds to lose it.

NEVER RIDE OFF: Brothers do not abandon their family.

ACKNOWLEDGEMENTS

In the past, I've asked if any of you actually take the time to read this part of the book. If you do, I thank you for you absolute dedication and I'd love to hear from you. BIG KISSES! Thank you to every single one of you who keep reading my words. I'm blown away by the love you show me!

For those of you who have read this stuff in the past, I apologize if the rest sounds redundant.

Kristin, my ride-or-die. I couldn't ask for a better PA or friend. Thank you for keeping me in line, boosting me up when I stumble, and working relentlessly to make my books successful. Love you more than you'll ever know.

Pam, I love you, Babe! Not only do you love my books, you are a loyal and true Beta. I cannot thank you enough for all the time you've spent on reading and relentless promoting my book babies. You're one of a kind.

A huge thank you to my family who brag about me being an author (despite the genre in which I write!) and for always believing in me. For my extended family, I do kind of wonder if you know exactly what I write, or if your friends read it and are traumatized.

If this is my first book you've read, you may not know who he is, but a huge thank you goes out to **PSH**, my very own "Porn Star Hubby" (if you ever meet me, or friend me on social media, ask me to tell you the story). You're the best book schlepper, one man cheerleading squad, and pimp-er of my books that ever walked the earth. Love you bunches.

Penny. YOU DID IT!!! Once upon a time there was a girl who didn't believe in herself. Then came a red-headed girl (who is now officially a graduate nurse!) that smacked the first girl upside the head and said, "You can do this!" Thank you for being a great friend and my unfailing supporter. You are never surprised at my success and *that* is humbling.

Lisa and **Brenda,** all those years ago, we met through our love of books and look where we are now! You invited me to join you at a book signing when I had no idea what they were (crazy, huh?). I had two books out and still didn't really know what I was doing. Your support, advice, and friendship have been priceless. I love you guys! Thank you for loving the fact that my mind is always moving and my characters take over at times.

Glenna, I cannot thank you enough! Because of you, Raptor's Revenge has a gorgeous cover. I look forward to working with you again on the rest of my RBMC boys! MUAH! (PSST! If y'all haven't read Glenna Maynard's books, you're missing out!)

Stacey of **Champagne Book Design,** I've said it before and I'll say it again… you are and forever will be a goddess! I'm so glad you made it to Shameless this year! Thank you for making my pages a work of art and for being so understanding of my "don't kill me" messages and emails. LMAO.

The ladies of **Kristine's Krazy Fangirls**, y'all are the best. You're the lovers of my books, the ones that I share my funny stories with, the ones who cheer me on when I'm struggling with a book I promised you, and I love you all to pieces! (((BIG HUGS)))! I can't thank you enough for your comments, your support, and your love of all things books. Come join us if you're not part of the group www.facebook.com/groups/kristineskrazyfangirls

Often, I try to spin the military into my books. This is for many reasons. Because of those reasons, my last, but never least, is a massive thank you to America's servicemen and women who protect our freedom on a daily basis. They do their duty, leaving their families for weeks, months, and years at a time, without asking for praise or thanks. I would also like to remind the readers that not all combat injuries are visible, nor do they heal easily. These silent, wicked injuries wreak havoc on their minds and hearts while we go about our days completely oblivious. Thank you all for your service.

OTHER BOOKS BY
KRISTINE ALLEN

Demented Sons MC Series - Iowa

Colton's Salvation

Mason's Resolution

Erik's Absolution

Kayde's Temptation

Snow's Addiction

Straight Wicked Series

Make Music With Me

Snare My Heart

No Treble Allowed

String Me Up

Demented Sons MC Series - Texas

Lock and Load

Styx and Stones

Smoke and Mirrors

Jax and Jokers

Got Your Six (Formerly in Remember Ryan Anthology)

RBMC - Ankeny Iowa
Voodoo

Angel

A Very Venom Christmas

Chains

Haunting Ghost

Charming Phoenix

Sabre

RBMC - Dallas Texas
Taming Raptor

Raptor's Revenge

Sparking Ares (Coming Soon!)

The Iced Series
Hooking

Tripping

Roughing

Holding

Fighting Love

Heels, Rhymes, & Nursery Crimes
Roses Are Red (RBMC connection)

Violets Are Blue (Coming Soon!)

Pinched and Cuffed Duet with M. Merin
The Weight of Honor

The Weight of Blood (by M. Merin)

ABOUT THE AUTHOR

Kristine Allen lives in beautiful Central Texas with her adoring husband. They have four brilliant, wacky, and wonderful children. She is surrounded by twenty-six acres, where her five horses, four dogs, and six cats run the place. She's a hockey addict and feeds that addiction with season tickets to the Texas Stars. Kristine realized her dream of becoming a contemporary romance author after years of reading books like they were going out of style and having her own stories running rampant through her head. She works as a night shift nurse, but in stolen moments, taps out ideas and storylines until they culminate in characters and plots that pull her readers in and keep them entranced for hours.

Reviews are the life blood of an indie author. If you enjoyed this story, please consider leaving a review on the sales channel of your choice, bookbub.com, goodreads.com, allauthor. com, or your favorite review platform, to share your experience with other interested readers. Thank you! <3

Follow Kristine on:

Facebook www.facebook.com/kristineallenauthor

Instagram www.instagram.com/_kristine_allen_

Twitter @KAllenAuthor

TikTok: www.tiktok.com/@kristineallenauthor

All Author www.kristineallen.allauthor.com

BookBub www.bookbub.com/authors/kristine-allen

Goodreads www.goodreads.com/kristineallenauthor

Webpage www.kristineallenauthor.com

Made in United States
North Haven, CT
28 December 2022

30307857R00078